THE WOMAN WHO LOST EVERYTHING

THE WARLORD – BOOK 3

BY M. D. COOPER

M. D. COOPER

SPECIAL THANKS
Just in Time (JIT) & Beta Reads

James Dean
Lisa L. Richman
Manie Kilian
Timothy Van Oosterwyk Bruyn
Gene Bryan

Cover Art by Ravven
Cover Design by Wooden Pen Press
Editing by Jen McDonnell

TABLE OF CONTENTS

M. D. COOPER

FOREWORD

Katrina's story is one that came at the behest of fans who wanted to know more about what she went through before reuniting with Tanis.

Though the events from the beginning of *The Woman Without a World* through to the end of this book only cover a few years of Katrina's search for the *Intrepid*, they are the crucible that shaped her into a person quite different than the one who stayed behind at Kapteyn's Star when the *Intrepid* left.

In this book, we'll see how she handles her new power as the ruler of the Midditerra System, and how that system handles her as well.

It is hard for any of us to imagine what Katrina has gone through. She was raised by a sociopathic father who chased a ship of refugees for fifty years, just to catch her and kill her companions.

She watched the people she sacrificed everything for eventually discard her after her husband died of old age, while she still had hundreds of years left to live.

In time she found love again, but then lost it after a short while—a time where she suffered brutal torment.

And now she is alone, in power, but without anyone she can trust to lean on. Katrina hardens her heart, wrapping herself in the armor of what "must" be done to preserve herself.

Though it may cost her what morality she has left, and perhaps her sanity as well.

M. D. Cooper
Danvers, 2018

PREVIOUSLY IN KATRINA'S JOURNEY...

In the last installments of The Warlord, we saw Katrina leave Kapteyn's Star in search of the ISS *Intrepid*, the colony ship that terraformed the world of Victoria and built the colony before leaving to continue its journey to New Eden.

Katrina and her ship's AI, Troy, searched in the darkness between the stars for years before finally stumbling upon the Kapteyn's Streamer. The Streamer is a supermassive thread of dark matter trailing behind Kapteyn's Star that creates a gravitational lensing effect similar to that of a wormhole.

Like a wormhole, it distorts time as well as space.

When Katrina and Troy exit the Streamer, they find themselves twenty light years beyond New Eden, and 4,500 years in the future.

The *Intrepid* is nowhere to be found.

They learn that in the intervening years, the level of technology has plummeted; though there have been two advances that were game changers. The first being artificial gravity, and the second, faster than light travel.

Katrina and Troy decide that the best route forward is to get their ship, the *Voyager*, upgraded with FTL capability so they can continue their search for the *Intrepid*.

Thus begins Katrina's adventure in the Bollam's World System, where she engages a repair vessel named the *Havermere* to fly out to the edge of the system and upgrade her ship with the graviton systems that will allow for FTL capability.

Much to Katrina's delight, she finds love with the *Havermere*'s crew chief, a woman named Juasa. However, others on the ship learn of Katrina's advanced technology and conspire to steal it from her.

They strike a deal with a group of pirates known as the Blackadder, and, in the end, Katrina and Juasa are captured and taken to the pirate's stronghold, a place called Revenence, on the world of Persia.

Persia lies within the Midditerra System, a place ruled by canton lords, and overseen by a powerful admiral named Lara, who ensures peace while levying a heavy tax.

Jace and Malorie, the pirates who have taken Katrina, try to learn her secrets (one of which being the location of her ship) through torture of her and Juasa, but eventually they escape, only to realize that Admiral Lara is also after them.

The previous story ends with Katrina having finally defeated Jace, Malorie, and Lara, but at a terrible cost. Her lover, Juasa, is dead, her ship is still missing, and she is all alone.

Although, she *has* just seized an empire....

THE COUNCIL
STELLAR DATE: 01.29.8512 (Adjusted Gregorian)
LOCATION: Blackadder shuttle
REGION: Persia, Midditerra System

Katrina didn't blame the canton leaders for not wanting to come to Farsa Station. She wouldn't, either, if she were in their shoes.

But that didn't make her feel any better about taking a trip down to Persia's surface; especially a trip that put her right in the biggest pit of vipers left in the Midditerra System.

"You look worried," Korin said from his seat across from her in the shuttle.

Katrina gave a small nod. "A bit, yes. The cantons may not have the strength of the MDF or the Blackadder, but frankly, neither do we anymore."

"Yeah." Korin glanced out the shuttle's window at the world of Persia below them. "We lost a lot of ships on both sides—and I think the remaining MDF ships would just as soon wipe out the Adders as look at them."

"That's why I've kept most of the MDF fleets in the outer system—even though we could really use their strength at Persia. If the canton lords—especially those who sat out the conflict—were to band together, they could crush what Blackadder vessels we have left."

Korin barked a laugh. "The day those dickheads all band together will be the day all the stars burn out. They couldn't agree on what to order for lunch."

"That's what I'm counting on." Katrina looked out the window at the growing world below them. "Hard to believe a system like this has a world like Persia. Place is like a paradise."

"If not for the people living on it." He tried to appear nonchalant, but Korin's tone belied the deep anger he felt for the cards life had dealt him.

Persia had not been a paradise for him.

Katrina decided to shift the conversation. "You know. I'd never been on a self-sustaining world around a G Class star until I woke up in Revenence Castle. We had a few nice worlds in Sirius, but the dog star does not cast a forgiving light. They had to use planetary rings to generate magnetic shields to keep the worlds safe. Victoria wasn't even that nice. It was self-sustaining, but there's something depressing about living in perpetual twilight."

Korin shook his head and gave her a wry smile. "Well, I've never been outside the Midditerra system. Stars, I've only been to the outer system twice in my life. With all you've seen, I'm—uh, nevermind."

Katrina was curious what Korin was going to say, but she suspected that not voicing it was the right choice. As far as she was concerned, her past was a mass of open wounds. The good memories seemed lost in the morass of bad ones.

"Think they'll all attend?" she asked, changing the subject completely this time.

Korin shrugged. "Well, Lord Troan of Canton Selkirk will—what, with us holding the council meeting in his city. Let's see, of the six cantons—other than Selkirk and the Blackadder—I expect we'll see Marion from Kurgise; at the very least, she'll want to know what your plans are. Canton Draus helped Jordan's ships in one of the engagements, plus we used MDF ships to keep raiders off one of their outer system stations, so I think you can count them as friends—so much as anyone can here."

"I spoke with Lady Armis of Draus earlier in the day," Katrina replied. "She said that she hates traveling to Selkirk—and Lord Troan in general—but is going to attend. I think at one point she was going to back out entirely, but I think she wants to see what my plans are."

"That's likely going to be the prevailing sentiment." Korin grabbed a bottle of water from the row of drinks tucked into pockets along the bulkhead. "Keep your enemies close, and all that."

"My sentiment entirely." Katrina let a hard smile slip onto her face and saw Korin's eyes narrow. "You don't approve?"

"I—honestly…I have no idea. Sure, it would be nice if everyone could just agree to get along. But I'm not stupid. I know that if you give any of those lords—even Armis—a meter, they'll take a light year."

"Or they'll drive a knife into my back," Katrina added.

"Yeah, not 'or', 'and'."

The shuttle shuddered as it dipped into Persia's atmosphere, racing over the western ocean. They were still a hundred kilometers up, and Katrina could see a breathtaking storm covering half the ocean, twisting its way east across the globe.

Flashes of lightning flared in the clouds, visible even in the daylight as it leapt across the towers of moisture stretching up toward space.

Katrina marveled at the beauty and considered that, even though humans could terraform planets, build massive stations, and construct nearly anything their hearts and minds desired, nature was still a wonder to behold.

In all honesty, humans really just nudged things. Took asteroids and dropped their water on planets. Encouraged atmospheres, planted life.

But they didn't invent any of it—they just replicated their homeworld over and over again. Sure, the details changed, but by and large, humanity was a species obsessed with recreating Earth in as many ways as possible.

Maybe it was all the more important now that Earth was a barren wasteland, destroyed by the Jovians in the Third Solar War in their vindictive hubris. There were, however, rumors that the AST was restoring humanity's homeworld, removing the radioactive soil, resurfacing the planet so they could seed life there once more.

Good luck, you bastards.

Katrina had no specific dislike for the AST, but the people of Sol hadn't batted an eye when Sirius destroyed the Kapteyn Primacy. Stars, they'd invited them into the Hegemony of Worlds not long after.

Alpha Centauri, Sol, and Tau Ceti, the three oldest bastions of humanity, were now the heart of the most malicious empire the species had ever known.

Katrina was just glad that Midditerra was over seventy light years from their border. Traders from the AST passed through Midditerra, but they were thankfully few and far between.

Star systems like Bollam's World worried her a lot more. They were only forty light years away. The Bollers could have a fleet in the thousands already on the way to Midditerra; with the cantons in disarray, and the Midditerra Defense Force down two fleets, she would need to forge all the alliances she could.

And then kill any who would not stand at her side. There was no room in her Midditerra System for dissenters.

The shuttle continued to drop, and Katrina caught sight of one of the fighters escorting the shuttle in. It was a stubby thing with a fanged mouth painted on the front—though with the carbon scoring, it was hard to make out most of the teeth.

There would be more of them out there. Jordan had dispatched seven of her best to come down with Katrina—not that the Adders had many fighters to speak of. Neither the MDF nor the Blackadder used a lot of single pilot fighters, or even NSAI drones, for that matter.

Which was why Jordan had the *Castigation* following along high above. If anyone wanted to destroy Katrina's shuttle, it would be the last thing they did.

Though Katrina hoped deterrence would work better than actual violence, which was why four other Blackadder heavy frigates were bracketing the *Castigation*.

13

It wasn't a huge force, and there were hundreds of other warships near Persia—less than half of which were loyal to Katrina—but her five ships were filled with crews who had proven themselves time and time again over the past week. The blood on their metaphoric swords was a deterrent in and of itself.

The shuttle eventually dropped into the clouds, passing through the storm with barely a shudder, the grav shielding protecting the ship from the storm's buffeting winds. After a few minutes of darkness surrounding the vessel, they burst free from the storm, moving into clear skies, continuing toward the western continent.

Katrina could see ships moving out from the seaports along the coast, returning to the fishing grounds now that the storm had passed. Beyond the coastal port cities were the rolling hills of Canton Selkirk, marching steadily up to the high peaks of the mountains that defined the region.

Selkirk City was deep in the mountains, an urban city consisting mostly of towering spires that filled a broad valley between two major ranges.

"Five minutes to touch down, Lady Katrina," the pilot called back. "We have priority clearance on tower pad A4."

The shuttle slowed as it passed over the hills and then the first of the peaks that made up the Presidia Range.

Katrina nodded absently as she stared out the window at the craggy mountaintops, most snow-capped and gleaming in the sunlight. Her HUD lit up, marking the locations of small towns and villages in the deep valleys, and she wondered what life was like for those people.

Selkirk was a capitalistic canton. As such, it was wealthier than many of the others, but that wealth was distributed between the leading business owners. From what Katrina had learned, Lord Troan liked to pretend as though he was the preeminent canton on Persia, but in reality, he was beholden to many of his internal supporters.

This made him weak and easy to exploit. All Katrina had to do was twist the knobs on Canton Selkirk's imports and exports, and the titans of commerce would demand that Lord Troan win her favor.

The break in the mountainous region came suddenly, the peaks falling away to reveal the Vale of Selkirk, a four-hundred-kilometer-long valley with a broad river running through it. Initially, the vale was lush and green, but it didn't take long to move into the city—which consumed nearly half of the valley.

There, tall spires of steel and gleaming glass stretched into the sky, some taller than the mountains around them. As they passed deeper into the city, the towers became denser and stretched higher, until the shuttle reached the tallest of them all: a skyscraper that reached over seven kilometers into the air.

"Think Lord Troan is compensating for something?" Korin chuckled as the pilot slowed for his final approach, circling the tower to land on Pad A4.

"Not sure why," Katrina said, amused by Korin's audacity more than the joke. "I hear a biomod can fix that pretty easily."

Korin snorted. "Maybe he got it made too big and doesn't know what to do with it now."

Katrina made a gagging sound. "I just had the worst mental image—that this entire tower is just his modded penis that he's showing off to the world."

"It may not have organic origins, but really, what else do you think this tower is?"

He had a point, and Katrina gave a sad shake of her head. "Great. Now I'm going to enjoy this little tête-à-tête even less. I'm docking a day from your pay."

"Wait…" Korin flashed a grin. "I get paid for this?"

"Funny."

The shuttle settled down, and Korin rose first, walking into the rear cabin to supervise the guards, who would secure the pad and the route to the meeting.

Katrina rose and stretched her arms, reveling in the burning sensation that raced down her sides, her nerves crying out at the movement, just as they had throbbed from sitting on the shuttle.

It was the price of her armored skin.

There was nothing for it. The risk of going under to repair the damage to her body was too great. Even those she trusted—as much as she was able—could turn on her, if she gave them such an opportunity.

Better to live with the agony; it wasn't too hard to ignore, after days on end. Once the *Voyager* finally found Midditerra, she would use its medical facilities to make her body whole again.

If Troy and the ship ever showed.

<Well, Malorie,> Katrina said as she reached down and grabbed the nondescript case next to her seat. <Time to

see what your council friends think of the change of management here in Midditerra.>

<I hate you,> Malorie growled. <With every fiber of my being, I want to see you destroyed.>

<Mal, is that any way to speak to the person who saved you? We've been over this. I could have let you die on the floor after you were shot. And I think I should remind you that your husband didn't rush to save you.>

<I wish you'd let me die. What am I now? I'm a...a thing, you've made me a monster.>

Katrina walked into the rear cabin, noting that the soldiers had left the area in spotless condition, something she would commend them for.

<You were always a monster, I just took away the deceptive body you wore. Now you have no beautiful disguise to hide behind. It's just your filthy mind, naked before me.>

Malorie didn't reply, but Katrina could feel the woman's rage and malice flowing over the Link.

Despite everything that had happened—the torture, the abuse—Katrina found herself liking Malorie more and more. The woman was resilient. A survivor, like herself. There was something powerful in the core of such a person that could not be easily dismissed.

Jace, however, was just a greed-driven, murdering monster. A creature with no redeeming qualities, who deliberately destroyed people for his own pleasure. Malorie had done that too, but she had been somewhat kind to Juasa during their imprisonment.

That counted for something.

Despite the woman's current condition, Katrina was still considering putting Malorie back in her place in

17

Revenence Castle. She was skilled at running the sithri operation, and, right now, Katrina needed all the revenue she could drum up.

If the sithri stopped flowing for too long, some other designer drug would fill the gap, and Katrina would have an uphill battle to regain Blackadder's former place.

The real question is in what fashion will she resume her place as the Lady of Revenence Castle, Katrina mused.

She could have Malorie ensconced in the castle in her current form, just a braincase on a pedestal. Or perhaps Malorie could have a body. Maybe an automaton's frame, or even something that appeared to be organic—if the woman learned to behave herself.

Korin had been given enough time to secure the landing pad; Katrina pushed her long coat back and checked the pair of pistols on her hips. She made sure they were loose in their holsters before stepping off the shuttle, into the bright Persian sunlight.

The two-dozen soldiers—all Blackadder assault commandos—had secured the platform, and a team was moving into the building to check the hallway inside.

Katrina nodded with approval before looking up to see two of the fighters circling high overhead.

"Tight as can be up here," Korin said before gesturing to a man standing near the building's entrance. "Troan's flunky there was a bit pissy about your soldiers going in first, but I told him it was our way or an orbital strike."

Katrina laughed. "You've been paying attention, Korin."

The man shrugged. "WWKD. What would Katrina do?"

"Don't take that too much to heart," Katrina replied, rapping a hand on her armor-sheathed chest. "I've made a few questionable decisions of late."

"Yeah, well, I draw the line at intentionally having my skin torn off my body." Korin gave a slight shudder as they walked toward the building's entrance, four of the Adders falling in around them.

"Well, if you recall, my skin was already half gone. You might have gone my route, if you were in that shape."

Korin shook his head. "I'd need balls as big as your breasts to pull something like that off."

"Well, balls typically don't survive that sort of rapid operation."

Korin sucked in a sharp breath. "Noted. WWKD with the distinct exception of body mods. In that case, choose the *opposite* of WWKD."

"Good call."

They'd held the conversation in front of Lord Troan's man, whose face had lightened in pallor as he waited for them to finish speaking.

"Lady Katrina," he swallowed after speaking the words. "You are most welcome in Canton Selkirk. You are in good hands here. There's no need for so many guards, or the fighters above."

"Are you sure?" Katrina asked.

"Yes, very, my Lady. You're quite safe here."

"What if I want to kill everyone and destroy the tower? If I don't have my ships and soldiers, that may take a while."

The man had gained a bit of color during the exchange, but it was gone again in an instant.

"My Lady?" he croaked.

Korin reached out and clasped a hand on the flunky's shoulder. "She's messing with you."

"Thank stars."

Korin's grin grew wider. "At least, Lady Katrina won't blow up the tower while she's in it. But when we leave…."

The man let out a shaky breath, and Katrina laughed. "See? I'm here, so you're perfectly safe. Now, are you going to stand there all day, or are we going into the council meeting?"

After another gulp and a nod, the man turned and led them into the building and down a corridor to a lift. Katrina inferred from the sign above the lift that they were on floor thirteen-eighty-two.

"Destination?" she asked the man.

"Uh…the meeting?"

"No, the floor," Korin elaborated.

"Oh…um, just three floors down."

Katrina saw a doorway to the staircase and nodded toward it. "We'll take the stairs."

Four of the Adders moved into the stairwell, and she waited for Korin to nod that they'd secured the landings and the destination level.

The flunky looked like he thought she was being paranoid, and he may have been right, but Katrina wasn't about to get into a lift seven kilometers in the air, in a building controlled by a man she had no reason to trust.

Just being in Troan's tower made her skin crawl...as much as it could.

When they arrived at floor thirteen-seventy-nine, Lord Troan was waiting for them, a look of clearly manufactured concern on his face as Katrina stepped out of the stairwell.

"Katrina, thank you for coming," he said, holding out his hand in greeting.

Three things struck her about Troan. The first was that he did not use any title when addressing her—he would likely contest her appropriation of the Blackadder's canton as one of his first orders of business. The second was that he was rather short, over thirty centimeters lower than her. The third was a momentary look of disappointment, or dismay.

*I think this bastard **did** have something planned for the lift. I bet his poor doorman would be saddened to know how expendable he was.*

Katrina doubted that Troan could have succeeded in killing her so easily. It takes a lift a long time to fall seven kilometers; enough time for her to reach into the tower's network and undo any sabotage that had been done.

Not that she really wanted to test that theory with her life.

"Lady Katrina," she said, folding her arms. She would not start this meeting with him thinking he was able to cow her.

"Excuse me?" Lord Troan asked.

Katrina eyed the two guards at Troan's back, and considered the placements of autoturrets on the ceiling.

There would be at least two, maybe three to fire into the stairwell if necessary.

Too many to deal with this quickly. She tamped down her anger, and gave the man a cold smile instead of the bullet she'd been contemplating.

"I am *Lady* Katrina, canton leader of Blackadder, and I am now the ruler of the Midditerra System. You may also call me 'Warlord' Katrina. 'Warlady' sounds a bit odd to my ears, and I'm not against letting the lesser gender get some peripheral benefit from association with me." She winked at the end, but Troan's scowl only deepened.

"The council determines who is the ruler of Midditerra. For centuries, the system ruler commanded the MDF—with a maximum strength not to exceed half the combined might of the cantons. As such, no canton leader can be the system ruler. It breaks the balance."

Katrina shrugged and walked past Troan. "Times change. By the way, next time you don't use my title, starfire falls on your city."

She strode down the corridor in the direction she assumed would lead to the meeting room while Troan rushed after her.

"That's not funny, Katr—" Troan stopped speaking as Katrina spun to face him, not bothering to disguise the disdain she felt for the despicable man.

"Do you think I play games, *Troan*?"

Troan shook his head, his lips curled into a snarl. "No, I've seen what you've done to the Midditerra System over the past few days. You stopped the fighting between the Adders and the MDF, but that doesn't give you the right to—"

"Which building?" Katrina asked.

"Pardon?" Troan stammered.

"The building. I'm going to let you pick. I told you I would drop starfire on your city. You pick where."

Troan's face drained of all color, as his eyes locked on hers. "You're serious," he whispered.

Katrina nodded. "I've sent a lot of people to die these last few days, and killed many more. What makes you think that I'll balk at this? I don't make idle threats. I say what I mean, and I won't be crossed. Pick. The. Building."

For a fraction of a second, a sly look came over Troan's face, then he nodded as though he was accepting of his punishment. "I understand. You have to do what you must. There is a factory on the western edge of town, at the base of Mount Hydra."

Katrina referenced her stored maps of Selkirk City. "The one owned by Omen Industries?"

Troan nodded slowly, a look of sorrow on his face. It was good—if she had no reason to distrust the man, she might have bought it.

Katrina pursed her lips as she regarded the slimy man before her. "Do you take me for a fool? I know that Omen is owned by your largest detractors of late. I'd be doing you a favor. But…what about the Litan Tower? It's just ten kilometers away, we could watch it fall from the council meeting room."

"The fuck?" Troan exclaimed, his carefully schooled expression fully disappearing for the first time. "You can't do that! It's in the middle of the city."

"And it's owned by Heras, one of your strongest supporters. I'll be sure to let her know that it was your indiscretion that caused her to lose one of her most prized assets."

Katrina placed her hands on her hips as she watched Troan try to decide what to do next. She could see that her Adders had all tensed, ready to take out the two Selkirk guards, who, for their part, looked as though they'd rather be anywhere else right then.

It seemed that Troan didn't inspire any particularly strong loyalty in his people.

The Adders, on the other hand, were loving every minute. Katrina's show was as much for them as it was to cow Troan. They would spread stories of her unbending strength amongst the troops.

Everyone liked being on the winning team.

"I'll give you an alternative," Katrina offered the struggling leader of Canton Selkirk.

"Yes?" he asked, hope appearing on his face.

"Get on your knees."

"My what?"

"Knees," Katrina sneered. "I assume you know what they are."

Lord Troan glanced at his guards, then at Korin and the Adders, realizing that he had no recourse—other than earning the unending animosity of Heras and the Litan family.

He eased down onto his knees, and Katrina held out her hand for him.

"Kiss it."

"What?" Troan looked up at Katrina, outrage mixing with fear.

"I've changed my mind. Korin, call Captain Jordan. Destroy Litan tower."

"No! I'll do it," Troan called out, then leant forward, lips pressed together.

Katrina stepped forward, put a hand on the back of Troan's head, and pressed his face into her crotch at the exact moment the lift doors opened, and Ladies Marion and Armis emerged.

Timed perfectly.

"Oh, glad you both were able to make it," Katrina said, lifting her hand off the startled Lord Troan's head and stepping back to reveal him on his knees, face turning the color of an overripe tomato. "Troan was just expressing his devotion to me in repayment for a recent transgression."

Lady Armis whistled and shook her head at Troan. "Lady Katrina has been here for five minutes. What could you have done already?"

Troan didn't speak as he struggled to his feet, but Katrina's leg shot out, and her knee slammed into his face, knocking him into the wall.

"Tell her, *Troan.*" Katrina emphasized the omission of his honorific. "Confession is a part of your penance."

Troan shot Katrina a worried look as he put a hand to his cheek. She could see understanding dawn on his face. He was dealing with someone who was not going to play by any of the rules he was accustomed to. She would respond with maximum force in all things, and would not back down. There would be no negotiating. No wheeling and dealing.

"I...I didn't use her title," Troan admitted quietly.

"Which is?" Katrina asked.

Troan looked down at her feet. "Lady Katrina."

"Excellent," Katrina replied, and turned away from the scene, resuming her walk down the hall to the council room. "That was a lot of work to get one specific word out of you, Troan."

The hall was short, and a moment later, she reached the double doors leading into the council chamber. They opened automatically, and Katrina strode into the oval room.

With glass walls on three sides, the meeting place was shaped like a clear egg, jutting out over the city far below. In the center rested a table, which was also crystal clear, with silver chairs surrounding it.

Katrina walked to the window and surveyed the city of Selkirk, spread out before them.

"It's impressive," she said, turning back to look at Troan and the two ladies as they entered the chamber. In the corridor, the Adders denied entrance to the other council members' guards and assistants.

"Umm...thank you, Lady Katrina," Troan said quietly. He was still nervous, trying to understand what had just happened to his standing.

One thing was certain: Lady Marion was enjoying Troan's discomfort, openly sneering at the man. Armis was more reserved. Katrina supposed the leader of

26

Canton Draus knew that anyone who behaved as Katrina was could easily turn her unbridled vengeance on friend as well as foe.

Something she should remember.

"Captain Jordan," Katrina called out audibly as she contacted the *Castigation* over the Link. "Fire on the beta target."

<*You got it, Lady Katrina,*> Jordan replied, her mental tone belying no angst over what she was about to do.

"What!?" Troan screamed, rushing toward Katrina, only to stop short as her arm snapped out, the barrel of her pistol pressed against his forehead.

"Watch," Katrina ordered.

The *Castigation* didn't possess beams powerful enough to penetrate through a hundred kilometers of atmosphere and do instant and catastrophic damage, so, despite the fact that Katrina had threatened starfire, the trio of rail-fired tungsten rounds that screamed toward the city would have to do.

They struck a site on the eastern edge of the city, debris and flames pouring into the sky in a great plume, followed by secondary explosions that pushed a great black cloud into the air.

The target was a manufacturing complex owned by Troan's ally, Heras. It was mostly automated and minimally staffed, making for few human casualties.

Not that Katrina was overly concerned. Maneuvering for power within the council was war. There were casualties in war.

Katrina sent a message to Heras of the Litan family, letting her know why she had been targeted, and trusted that Jordan would coordinate cleanup with the city's management.

"Do you understand your position?" Katrina asked Troan, her pistol still pressed against his forehead.

The man nodded slowly, eyes fixed on her trigger finger. "I do."

"Good, now send a message to all of your ships and military assets instructing them to stand down."

Katrina could have done it on his behalf—she'd planted nano on him when she had pressed his face against her steel gusset—but she wanted to see if he would do it of his own volition and listened in on his Link connection.

<General Vedre, do not respond to the Adder ships. Inform everyone to stand down.>

<Lord Troa—>

<Just do it!> Troan ordered his general.

"It's done," he said aloud, all the fight gone out of him. "May I sit, Lady Katrina?"

Katrina nodded as she watched emergency response vessels race across the city to the site of the orbital strikes, a tightening in her chest threatening to ruin her resolve.

"You may."

* * * * *

Katrina did not speak further until the rest of the canton lords and ladies arrived. For their part, Persia's leadership spoke in muted tones, giving Katrina sidelong looks from time to time.

She imagined that much of their chatter was occurring over the Link. Except for Troan. He wasn't talking to anyone—other than to suffer an abusive tirade from Heras of the Litan family over the loss of their facility.

A small part of Katrina felt bad for the man. He had probably begun the day with high hopes of establishing his position with her—or perhaps over her. Now he was likely wondering if he would even possess his canton by the time night fell.

Unless he did something stupid, Katrina had no intention of stripping it from him. She had already made the effort to turn him into her pawn. It would be foolish to waste that and have to repeat the process with his successor.

ORDERS
STELLAR DATE: 01.03.8512 (Adjusted Gregorian)
LOCATION: Genchuta Station
REGION: Corona, Bollam's World System (58 Eridani)

Admiral Pierson stared at the report that hovered in the air over his desk. At first he'd wondered if General Yves of the Intelligence Directorate was messing with him. It would be just the thing Yves would do.

Guy thinks he's such a comedian. How he runs the BWID is beyond me.

But this report did not appear to be faked. Blackadder ships were definitely searching for something, which meant that they did not capture the Streamer Woman's ship at the edge of the Bollam's World System, as the investigators had first believed.

It was still out there somewhere.

Of course, that was little help. With over ten thousand settled stars within two months' travel, it was entirely possible for a ship to disappear forever.

So why is the Blackadder searching at all?

Pierson leant back in his chair and ran a hand through his short grey hair. There *had* been some fighting between the ships at the edge of the system before the Blackadder made off with the *Havermere*.

It was *possible* that they had captured someone from the Streamer Woman's ship...or maybe even the woman herself. That would explain why the pirates thought the Streamer ship would still be nearby.

Conversely, the pirates could just be stupid.

Pierson pushed the report from the BWID to the side and pulled up the Omicron-9 strategic assessment.

The assessment was old, from one of the Omicron war games that the Bollam's World Space Force had participated in a few decades past. It was a simulated assault on a system very much like Midditerra.

For decades, the pirates that operated out of Midditerra had been a thorn in the side of surrounding star systems. Though Bollam's World was on the periphery of the Midditerra System's reach, they had joined in the multi-system Omicron war games to see how other nearby militaries operated, as much as to practice an attack on Midditerra.

The problem with the Midditerrans was that they were more than just a band of outlaws who had managed to hold onto a star system for a few years. Within Midditerra, they lived under the rule of law— mostly. They had their canton lords, and their Defense Force.

In an all-out attack, Bollam's World would certainly win against the MDF, but it would be costly. Half of the civilian ships within Midditerra were privateers that were nearly as well armed as destroyers.

It would be impossible to tell who was friend, foe, or innocent bystander.

Which was, of course, the reason why no one had yet tried to take out Midditerra. The cost just wasn't worth the gain.

Though that may have finally changed.

<Admiral Pierson,> a voice came into his mind, and the admiral restrained himself from groaning.

31

<President Amalia, how wonderful to hear from you this afternoon. How are you?>

<I'm pissed, Pierson, that's what I am. Transfer this to holo, I want to see you.>

Pierson rose from his chair and walked across his office to an open space in front of a window looking over the Genchuta Space Station. He made sure his uniform appeared crisp, and then put the president on the holoview.

The president appeared, wearing a white skinsuit that seemed to be on fire, blue-white flames licking their way up her body. Pierson wondered if that's what she really was wearing, or if she was simply presenting herself that way on the holo.

He was grateful that his position in the military allowed him to forego the ridiculous fashions that forever occupied the elites.

"President Amalia, you look resplendent. What has you so upset?"

Amalia leveled a finger at him, jabbing it over and over as she spoke. "Don't fuck with me, Pierson. You got the same report I did about the Streamer Woman. General Yves thinks her ship is still nearby."

"Yes, he does," Pierson nodded. "Yves suspects many things, many of which turn out to be wrong, or are not actionable in any useful way. This could well be both."

"I don't care, Pierson. You saw the spectrographic analysis, just like I did. That ship was manufactured at Kapteyn's Star, and it made an FTL jump just hours after the KSS repair ship reached it. If that's not Golden Age tech, then nothing is."

Pierson nodded. The president was right about that. The fact that the Streamer ship had made an FTL jump was unprecedented. No other ship that had come out of Kapteyn's Streamer had ever managed such a feat—that they knew of.

Which made it all the more likely that searching for the ship was a fool's errand.

"I want you to prepare a plan for how we can take the Midditerra System," President Amalia said when Pierson didn't respond. "Those pirates either have the ship, or have clues as to its whereabouts."

Pierson held back a sigh. "I can contact the other systems that participated in the Omicron—"

"No." The president's hand sliced through the air. "No one else. Just us. I don't plan to share whatever we learn with any other systems. Stars, half of our allies would cut and run as soon as they had the intel."

Pierson pursed his lips, nodding thoughtfully. He was in agreement with that assessment, which is why he was against the entire venture. "We can't take the system alone. Not unless we want to leave our own unprotected."

"Alter the rules of engagement, Admiral. Everyone in Midditerra can be declared an enemy of our state. Stars, if they're not actively pirating, they're in league with them, anyway."

"And all their slaves and indentured workers?"

"Obviously you won't need to target them, but if they are killed? Well, every war has its casualties."

Pierson clenched his teeth. *It's easy for President Amalia to say that.* She could stay in her opulent offices and dispatch soldiers to kill for her; never seeing the real cost of war, only reaping the benefit of the technology they secured.

Still, one thing was for certain: if the Streamer Woman did have Golden Age tech, there were few worse outcomes than the pirates of the Midditerra System getting their hands on it.

Pierson gave the president a slow nod. "Very well. We'll put together a modified plan where we do a lightning strike on the Midditerra System. I can have it ready for you—"

"Today, Admiral Pierson. You'll have it for me today."

"Of course, President Amalia."

The holo snapped off, and Admiral Pierson turned and stared out the window, taking deep breaths as he tried to regain his composure.

How many of the men and women under his command would die because of Amalia's impatience?

<Charlie,> he called out to the fleet's administrative AI. <Assemble the command team on the double. We have a strategy to form.>

<For taking Midditerra?> Charlie asked.

Pierson chuckled. <Listening in?>

<No, I got the report from Yves, as well. Looks like he's trying to railroad you into action.>

<Well, it worked. We convene in thirty minutes.>

<Very good, sir.>

Pierson returned his attention to the scene outside his window, watching as a cruiser, the *Ark of Truth*, pulled away from the station.

A thousand men and women were on that ship. Soldiers, techs, naval personnel. They had no way of knowing that their ship was now just weeks away from war.

But they would soon.

DEMONSTRATION

STELLAR DATE: 01.29.8512 (Adjusted Gregorian)
LOCATION: Selkirk City
REGION: Canton Selkirk, Persia, Midditerra System

She continued to stand at the window, staring out over the city, until the last canton lord—Derrick of Pellese—sat at the table. Then she turned to survey them.

Including her, they were the eight lords of the Cantons of Persia. And though technically they had no official power in the far reaches of the system, all had many holdings beyond the central world of the Midditerra System.

Only two or three people in the system had power that matched the canton lords, but they were situated in the outer regions of Midditerra—regions Katrina would have to visit soon.

When push came to shove, the canton rulers selected the leader of the Midditerra Defense Force, and that leader—though a power in his or her own right—served at the pleasure of the council.

Until now.

"I'm glad you all came," Katrina said. "You should be happy I'm here, too—it means I'm not going to call starfire down on this building, like I did on that unfortunate factory."

No one laughed at her statement, every person wondering if she would actually have destroyed Troan's tower if she hadn't come.

Maybe she would have. Yesterday, when speaking with Jordan, she had considered that very thing. But since her conversation with Armis earlier in the day, Katrina had decided that keeping as much of the current power structure in place was in her best interests.

Provided she could control the key players—though that did not mean every person present would survive the council meeting.

"Honestly, it's no less than some of you deserve. Most of you sat out the conflict between the Blackadder and the MDF. If I hadn't stepped in, they would have destroyed one another. Granted, that's probably what a few of you—" she glanced at Troan "—were hoping for."

The lord of Canton Selkirk didn't meet her gaze, and a few more found other things to look at, as well. Armis's gaze didn't waver, and Katrina was glad to have a solid ally.

"It is not the place of the cantons to get involved in a dispute between a particular canton and the MDF," Lady Marion said, her tone unwavering, though she did glance at Lord Wills of Canton Arison.

"I've heard this," Katrina replied. "Historically, you haven't done it because it's the right thing to do. You sat out past conflicts for the same reason you did these past few days. You want to wear down whichever canton is at odds with the MDF—maybe the MDF as well—so you can prop up a new ruler.

"Speaking of which, we need a better name than 'ruler'. Makes me feel like I'm used for measuring things. I've been debating 'Queen' or 'Empress', but I don't want to be too pretentious, so you can call me 'Warlord

Katrina'. Though I won't blow up your cities if you only call me 'Lady Katrina'."

"I don't think that's very funny," Lord Wills said quietly, his eyes narrowing. "You just killed a hundred people, just to make a point to Troan, here."

"Eighty-seven," Katrina corrected him, her tone even. "How many slaves did you sell last week, Lord Wills? How many of the poor in your canton serve as living organ farms for the rich? Or what about when you sabotaged and destroyed Lady Marion's research facility that was studying the use of neutronium for quantum computers?"

"What the hell?" Marion half rose from her chair, turning to Wills. "That was you?"

Wills shook his head. "I had nothing to do with that. She's just trying to rile us up. Pit us against one another."

Katrina rested her elbows on the table and leant forward. "I know everything Lara knew. I also have all of Jace and Malorie's intelligence. Good thing for the rest of you that they didn't get along; between the three of them, they have serious dirt on each and every one of you. Tell them, Malorie."

Katrina picked up Malorie's case and set it on the table. There was a brief pause, but then Malorie spoke, her voice emanating from the braincase.

"It's true, she has stripped a lot of information from our minds. Lara's too. I suppose knowing that some of you are going to suffer mightily is a small silver lining for what's become of me."

"Shit," Lady Marion whispered. "Mal?"

"Yeah, Marion, you dimwitted fool. It's me, Malorie. You know what I know about you, so you should probably just shut your mouth and—no, actually, be your usual self. I'd like to see you in a braincase next to me."

Malorie's voice dripped with venom, yet sounded gleeful at the mention of Marion suffering.

Marion's mouth snapped shut, but her eyes were wide and staring. Katrina noticed that Wills was smiling as he regarded Malorie's brain case, but the rest of the council members glanced at one another, expressions of worry lining their faces.

"So, Lord Wills." Katrina stared the man down. "Shall we look at the evidence that says you were behind the attack on Marion's facility?"

"I sure would like to," Marion said quietly, worry over a misstep losing to the desire for vengeance.

"Don't be so hasty," Katrina turned to Marion. "You're not blameless. Why, just a few—"

"OK!" Marion held up her hands. "We get the picture."

"Pity," Lord Derrick grinned at Marion. "I was at least curious to know how long ago Wills had taken out your facility. A few misfortunes have befallen me of late that I'd like to know about, as well."

"I didn't—" Wills began, but Katrina cut him off.

"You did. I have the evidence, and I think I'll turn it over to Marion later…or maybe I'll just tax you on what I expect your ventures will make, with her facility out of the way."

"You're ascendency is quite the misfortune in and of itself, Lady Katrina," Wills muttered.

"Well, you're going to meet some more," Katrina replied. She decided to push Wills further before she taught him a lesson. "I want each of you to turn twenty-five ships over to me. The MDF needs to be as powerful as half the cantons, and after the battles with Jace's loyalist ships, we're out of balance."

"That ratio is not meant to be a minimum requirement," Lady Jeshis of Canton Ulma blurted out, then clamped her mouth shut.

"Where are your manners?" Katrina asked.

"Um, I'm sorry."

Katrina held out her hand, palm up. "I'm sorry...."

"Warlord Katrina," Lady Jeshis said quickly.

"Mark my words." Katrina rose from her chair and paced along the length of the room. "With this recent unrest, we are a ripe target. Midditerra must strengthen its borders, and its resolve. I want all of your military leadership to send top-ranking liaisons to Farsa Station. We must form a unified front to ensure that our sovereignty is not undermined."

"We already have liaisons on Farsa, Lady Katrina," Lord Derrick explained. "What do you mean by 'top-ranking'?"

"I mean I want colonels or generals," Katrina replied. "Some of you have sent the lowest ranking officers you can. Others have sent spies. Plus, several of your liaisons fled Farsa during the fighting—not that I blame them."

Katrina turned and saw Lord Wills shooting daggers at her with his eyes, his fists clenching and unclenching.

"You don't like me, do you, Wills?"

"No," he breathed the response.

"Why not? I stopped the fighting between the MDF and the Adders. I'm protecting this system."

Katrina could see that the other lords and ladies were paying rapt attention to Wills. Several of them wore expressions of support, though most were schooled to be blank.

"You named yourself the ruler of Midditerra. That is not your place. The council—"

"In all fairness," Katrina interrupted, a smirk on her lips, "I named myself Warlord."

"Don't play your stupid semantics game with me," Lord Wills shot back. "You don't intimidate me."

Katrina glanced at Korin, who stood by the door, scowling at Wills. "Korin, stand down." She returned her gaze to Lord Wills. "Well then, kill me. Take control of the Midditerra System for yourself. It's what you want."

Wills didn't reply as he rose and walked toward her, his gaze sliding up and down her body.

"A test of arms or strength?" he asked.

"Whichever you prefer," Katrina replied.

"Strength, then," Wills said, and nodded to the pistols on Katrina's hips.

"Korin," Katrina said with a nod to the man. He approached as she took off her jacket, unbelted her holsters, and handed them over.

"You'd fight me in armor, while I have none?" Wills asked.

"For starters, it doesn't come off," Katrina replied. "Additionally, you're not an honorable man, so what do you care?

"You're right," Wills snarled, and a lightwand suddenly appeared in his hand as he lunged at Katrina.

She dodged the strike, Wills' glowing electron-blade stopping centimeters from her left cheek. He attempted to flick his wrist and slash the blade across her face, but Katrina slammed the heel of her hand into his wrist.

Wills' arm swung wide, but he held onto the electron blade.

"You're fast, Katrina," he whispered. "But it won't be enough."

He attacked again, slashing in short, controlled strikes, forcing Katrina to backpedal until she was only a meter from the clear wall of the oval room.

Wills lunged at her again, this time aiming for her chest.

Katrina twisted to the left, his electron blade passing between her chest and right arm, which she clamped together while driving the heel of her left hand into his nose, the hard steel smashing cartilage and bone.

Wills cried out and tried to fall back, but she held his arm fast. He tugged twice, and then she drove a knee into his groin, finally hearing the electron blade fall from his grip.

She released her hold on his arm and turned to find the blade still active, buried to the hilt in the clear floor.

Katrina dropped a thread of nano onto it, checking for a biolock failsafe—there was one—and disabling it before she picked up the lightwand.

"Turnabout is fair play, right?" She glanced at the other lords and ladies to see expressions of concern on their faces.

All except for Marion, who smirked at Wills as he knelt on the floor, one hand between his legs, and the other on his face.

Armis shrugged. "He brought this on himself. Wills' reach always did exceed his grasp."

Lord Wills struggled to his feet and brought his hands up, ready to reengage, even as blood poured from his nose, and tears streamed from his eyes.

"Good, Wills." Katrina nodded in satisfaction. "You'll at least die a little more honorably than you lived."

Wills cried out and threw a punch that Katrina knocked aside. He twisted and kicked at her waist, but she saw the move coming and pivoted, delivering her own kick into the knee of the leg he was standing on.

The bone cracked, and Wills screamed as he collapsed.

Katrina wasted no further time. She lunged forward, landing on his chest with her left knee, cracking his ribs, before slamming the lightwand into the side of his head.

She stood to survey her kill.

Wills' body convulsed like a flag in a hurricane for over twenty seconds, as smoke poured from his head, the smell of burning brains, skin, and hair filling the room.

Katrina watched expressions ranging from horror, to morbid curiosity, to glee—in Lady Marion's case—cross the faces of the council members.

Finally, she knelt at Wills' side and pulled the lightwand free.

"Been a while since I used one of these," she said, deactivating the blade. "Glad to see I haven't lost my touch."

No one spoke as Katrina returned to her seat. She placed the lightwand hilt on the table before her, then leaned back in her seat.

"Troan, make yourself useful and contact Lord Wills' heir. His daughter, I believe. Tell her she needs to be here in forty minutes to swear fealty to me, or I'll pay her canton a personal visit."

"Yes, Warlord Katrina."

"You all look so shocked," Katrina said, a grin splitting her lips. "Your veneer of civilization has always been just that—a thin skin over your rotten core. I'm here to be a new kind of ruler for Midditerra. The kind it deserves. And this begins with each of you swearing fealty to me."

"Are you serious?" Jeshis asked.

Katrina shrugged. "Want to ask Wills? I can arrange a meeting between the two of you in the afterlife."

* * * * *

The council had all sworn their fealty, named the ships they were turning over to the MDF, and selected their new liaisons.

Now considerably less happy than when they had entered, they were filing out of the room, dismissed by Katrina when she had no further need for them.

"Armis," Katrina called out to the Lady of Canton Draus. "A moment."

Armis turned from Lady Marion, touching her on the shoulder and sharing a look before walking back to Katrina.

"Yes, Warlord?"

"Despite our previous conversations, you were not as supportive as I had expected," Katrina said without preamble. "I got the distinct impression that you were waiting for me to slip up."

Armis nodded, her expression grave. "That's because I was. I did not encourage you to hold this meeting because I wanted to fawn over you, but because I wanted to see what you were made of."

Katrina searched Armis's face, scouring the other woman's visage for insight. There was not much to be found; Armis gave little of her internal thoughts away.

"And?" Katrina asked.

"And I think you'll be a sufficient guardian for the Midditerra System. But I don't like you."

For some reason, the way she said it struck Katrina as amusing, and she couldn't help but laugh.

"Well, that's too bad, Armis. I like you. And trust me, none of this is by my choice, but I'm not going to be a victim of circumstance. I'll control my destiny, thank you very much."

"And that of those around you?"

"You don't like the way I do things? Unseat me."

Armis's eyes narrowed as she regarded Katrina, and Katrina considered placing a neural lace in the woman's mind. Armis was clearly the most formidable of the council members. She understood when to bide her time, and when to strike.

Katrina respected that.

If she could turn the woman into a true ally, she'd be far more valuable than as a puppet.

"Maybe someday, Warlord," Armis said, a genuine smile appearing on her lips for a moment. "For now, we'll see how things play out."

"Thanks for your vote of confidence."

Armis laughed as she turned to leave the room. "Vote of something, at least."

AN ALLY'S ENEMY
STELLAR DATE: 01.29.8512 (Adjusted Gregorian)
LOCATION: Selkirk City
REGION: Canton Selkirk, Persia, Midditerra System

Armis sighed as she entered the lift, her two guards and assistant joining her. Katrina had behaved like a wild animal, possessing no restraint. Her words dripped with threats, and her actions were worse.

It was as though she were the worst possible combination of Jace and Lara put together into one person.

Days like this, I hate you, father. Well, hate you more, at least.

She was trying to build a better future for her people, but how was that even possible when she lived in such a cesspool—one filled with piranhas? Her father had been like the others, a despicable Lord of the Canton, who abused his people and took what he wished from them.

Somehow—through a process Armis had never fully fathomed—she had gained a different worldview. One where she had come to believe it was her place to protect and guide her people.

It was slow, arduous work, elevating her canton while taking care not to make it appear too weak or too juicy a target for the others. She also had to be cautious of how much her canton was viewed as a safe haven by the people of Persia.

If Canton Draus shared borders with the others, she would surely see hordes of refugees pour in each year.

As it was, even though Draus was a canton spread across a vast archipelago of islands, they still saw hundreds of people attempt daring ocean crossings each year.

"Glad to see that you survived the council session," Tal, her aide, said after a moment of silence. "I just about puked when they carried Lord Wills out."

"You and me both," Armis replied. "Katrina is a brutal monster."

"She's in pain," Tal said. "So much pain. Can't you see it in her eyes?"

Armis shrugged. "I do, but that doesn't matter." She opened her mouth to say more, but decided not to. Her scans showed no listening devices in the lift—not any more, at least—but Katrina possessed technology far beyond theirs. It was possible that she could be listening to them even now.

They exited the lift a moment later and walked down a short hall to shuttle pad A7. Armis forced herself to walk slowly, though she felt as though a target was on her back the whole way.

In the distance, smoke still rose from the location of Katrina's orbital strike, the haze drifting across the city, forming a grey film over the valley.

Once on the shuttle, Armis collapsed into one of the deep chairs and snapped her fingers for an automaton to bring her a glass of wine.

"Stars," she whispered after she took her first drink. "I had hoped to find a true ally in Katrina; someone who would help. And we were getting so close to unseating Lara, too. Just another month, and all the pieces would have been in place."

"Many of the assets are still in position," Tal replied as she settled in across from Armis. "It may take a bit longer, but we can use them against Katrina."

Armis shook her head. "No, let's not be so hasty. She did something to Troan. Something beyond the humiliation she subjected him to."

"Like what? She can't have sex—from what I hear, her body is a ruin under her metal skin. She's not controlling him that way."

Armis chuckled. "Katrina may be a crass, murdering bitch, but she doesn't need to resort to her womanly wiles to bend someone to her will."

"You're referring to the rumors about mind control?"

"Those would be the ones."

Tal shook her head, giving Armis the same amused look of mock-worry she had used since they were kids. "That's just conjecture."

"We have firsthand accounts of Katrina in Lara's presence, but Lara seemed subservient to *her*. Witnesses place Malorie on Farsa, too—though Katrina claims that Malorie and Jace were running their operations from Rockhall, while she was being held by Lara on Farsa—until Malorie managed to break free."

"But you don't believe it," Tal prompted.

Armis shrugged. "There are discrepancies in the timeline. You've noted some of them."

"Yeah, but there are other explanations," Tal replied, grinning and waving her hands in the air. "We don't need mystical mind control to explain it."

Armis laughed. Tal always had a way of getting a smile out of her when she was down. "You should look at the sort of tech they had back in the Golden Age. If Katrina is a Streamer like she claims, then she might as well have 'mystical mind control'. I watched her clear the biolock on Wills' lightwand in seconds. That's not something anyone here can do."

"She could be from the AST. They have tech like that—or so I've heard."

Armis raised her eyebrows. That was possible, though it changed little.

"Well, her origins aside, she's dangerous, and we'll have to play our cards carefully. Katrina went from being completely unknown to controlling an entire star system in under a week. That makes her the most dangerous person I know of."

"So what's our next move?" Tal asked.

Armis blew out a long breath. "I have *no* idea."

LIES AND VERISIMILITUDE
STELLAR DATE: 01.31.8512 (Adjusted Gregorian)
LOCATION: Katrina's quarters
REGION: Farsa Station, Persia, Midditerra System

Katrina hated sleeping.

Even with Korin and loyal Adders guarding her, she knew it was when she was the most vulnerable. Always having to be on guard, always having to portray this persona of absolute strength…it was harder than she thought it would be.

When she'd 'killed' Jace and taken Lara's place as the ruler of Midditerra, she thought that she could actually *be* the ruthless ruler. That Katrina the Warlord was who she had become.

She had thought she could be OK with that.

Instead, she felt like she was covered by a sheen of oil at all times, slick and stinking.

What Katrina longed for was a true confidant. But Juasa was dead, and Troy was still missing. The *only* person she had that could really understand her position was Malorie.

Malorie's braincase was near her bed; she'd not taken it back to her throne room to rejoin Jace, Lara, and Captain Hana. Katrina regarded it for a moment, wondering if reaching out to Malorie for companionship was a sign that she was losing her mind.

<Are you awake, Malorie?>

<Fuck you, Katrina.>

<I suppose I probably deserve that,> Katrina replied with a self-deprecating laugh.

<I don't even know if I sleep anymore. It's like everything is just a disjointed dream. I can't even tell if you're real.>

Katrina knew why that was. Malorie's brain wanted stimulation. However, because Katrina didn't want the woman to have access to outside nets, or even visuals, the braincase provided faux sensory input for Malorie's mind.

But it wasn't enough to make her feel grounded—especially for an L0 brain like Malorie's. It did, however, keep her from going stark raving mad.

<I've been thinking about that. I want you to know that I didn't intend this for you—I know you're as much a victim of all this as I was.>

Malorie made a derisive sound in her mind. <I'm no one's victim.>

<Liar. You were Jace's creature, and you know it.> Katrina paused, wondering if she should give Malorie a lifeline. <I was going to give you Revenence back, you know. Juasa and I had talked about it.>

<Now who's the liar? You would never have done that. You hate me.>

<Maybe. Juasa didn't, though.>

Katrina didn't know why she kept talking about Juasa. She'd been trying not to; it just hurt too much. Ju had so much of her life left to live. That fateful meeting with Katrina in the bar at Bollam's World had been the beginning of the end for her.

<I had a fondness for Juasa. I guess that is something we have in common,> Malorie replied.

<Would you like a body again?>

Katrina blurted out the question. What she *really* wanted was a friend. She thought Armis might have been a candidate, but she had been cold as ice in person.

How low have I sunk that I'm seeking friendship from **Malorie**?

Katrina wanted to scream, to rail against the universe, against Markus for being a stubborn old fool and dying on her, at Tanis for leaving her behind, at the people of the Primacy for casting her aside, at the Sirians for destroying everything.

At her father for being a raging asshole that had murdered people on a whim and then asked what was for dinner.

I guess the apple doesn't fall far from the tree....

Malorie didn't reply right away, but when she did, the words dripped with acid. *<I repeat, Katrina, fuck you.>*

<Is that any way to treat me after such a generous offer? I mean...you had my lover whip me till skin hung off my back in strips. The fact that I don't torture you continually should make you a little bit grateful.>

<Katrina, you are torturing me continually.>

<Well, I'm offering you your life back. A life without Jace's control. A chance to be your own woman.>

<Just trading one master for another,> Malorie replied coolly. *<Don't try to pretend it would be anything else.>*

<Fine, stay in the braincase. But you'll probably go insane in a few months. Or you can have a body.>

Katrina could feel Malorie fuming silently, likely considering her options. They were few: go mad, or take the offer. Suicide may have been a possibility, as well.

Katrina had heard stories of braincases that had suicided.

<What kind of body?> Malorie eventually asked.

<A robotic one of some sort, I imagine. I suppose down the road it could be organic—right now we don't have the resources to grow you a nice new fleshy bod.>

<Like an automaton?> Malorie's voice was hesitant.

<Sure, yeah. I get the feeling you have something in mind.>

<Well, back before we started using human pickers for the fields—you know, the whole 'handcrafted' thing—we used robotic pickers. Problem was, the NSAI just didn't have the skill to make some of the finer judgments as to which plants were ready and which weren't.>

Katrina was starting get an idea as to where this was going. <You had braincase pickers for a while.>

<Yes. We should still have some of their frames in storage at Revenence Castle.>

<Why do you want some sort of harvester machine to be your body?>

Malorie sighed. <I don't know. I suppose because I know that they're available, and they were both tough and graceful.>

<OK,> Katrina replied. <I'll reach out to Demy and see if she can ferret them out.>

<Tell her to ask Tom, the medtech. He'll know where they're stored.>

<OK.>

Katrina considered granting Malorie enough network access to handle the appropriation of her new body on her own, but decided that it would be best to put that off a little bit longer.

There was trust, and then there was trust.

* * * * *

Katrina had reached out to Demy—who was not sleeping, either. Though it was because she was working on repairs to the *Castigation*. The engineering chief agreed to get on the case, though she did not sound overjoyed at the prospect of providing Malorie with a body once more.

After going back and forth on potential control mechanisms and kill systems to keep Malorie in check, Katrina had left Demy with the details, and finally began to drift off to sleep.

<Warlord Katrina!> Jordan's voice broke into her mind, using an emergency code.

<What is it, Jordan?> Katrina asked.

She was about to tell Jordan that whatever news she had best be worth waking her up, but then she hoped it actually wasn't.

Let it be something stupid so I can actually sleep.

<It's Jace's flagship, the Verisimilitude. *It's docked at Nesella Station.>*

Katrina very nearly bolted upright in her bed. The *Verisimilitude* was a well-equipped cruiser that had evaded capture, and had not come in when the Adders loyal to Jace surrendered three days ago.

It had fled into the outer reaches of the system, leading Katrina to wonder if its first mate, a slimy man named Leon, had taken the ship and run. But if it was docked at Nesella Station, that was a horse of a different color indeed.

She pulled herself to her feet and walked into the san. *<Get your crew ready, Jordan. We'll be paying Nesella Station a little visit. I'll be on your ship in thirty minutes.>*

<Understood, Warlord.>

Nesella Station was the domain of a man named Kruger, one of the more powerful figures in the outer Midditerra System. He ran many of the stations that managed interstellar trade, at which the cantons operated their front businesses that sold stolen goods as though they were legitimate wares.

By mutual agreement, stations like Nesella were neutral ground, places where the cantons held no official power. They were run by the stationmasters with as little canton influence as possible, and protected by the MDF.

However, Katrina had learned from plumbing the minds of her captives that most of the 'free stations' were in the pocket of one or another of the canton rulers. There were a few exceptions, and the stations run by Kruger were amongst those.

Kruger was a ruthless man who ruled with an iron fist. He even had his own small 'security fleet', and during the recent unrest, no one had even attempted to raid his stations.

Although Kruger was not in the pocket of any canton leader, there were still those with whom he was more closely affiliated. Cantons who had special privileges on his stations.

From what Katrina had learned, Canton Kurgise was one that he was particularly close to—or maybe it was just Lady Marion that he shared a relationship with.

That the *Verisimilitude* would dock at Nesella was very telling. It reinforced Katrina's resolve to annex Kurgise for the Blackadder Canton.

But first, she wanted that ship. It was easily a match for the most powerful MDF cruisers and could be a key vessel in any system defense. It would also help balance the power between the Adders and the MDF.

Once her mods had completed their cycles, Katrina left the san, grabbed her coat, pistols, and turned to eye Malorie's case.

<Too bad you don't have your new body yet, I might be able to use you on this mission,> Katrina said to the black cylinder resting beside her bed.

<What mission?> Malorie asked.

<We're going to Nesella to secure the Verisimilitude,*>* Katrina said, her tone resolute. Destruction was an option, but she would greatly prefer to capture it.

<Shit, Katrina. You're going into the lion's den. You'll need me.>

<Why?>

<I know Kruger, and I know the Verisimilitude's *mate, Leon. If he's gone to meet with Kruger. You know what that means.>*

Katrina nodded—though Malorie could not see it. *<It's possible that he's allying with Marion of Kurgise. It's **also** possible that he's low on fuel and felt that Nesella would be a safe haven.>*

<You're not really that naïve, are you?>

*<Not really, no. But it **is** possible.>*

Malorie snorted. <*Even if he was low on fuel, you know he picked his gas station carefully. It wasn't a random selection.*>

<*Fine, Malorie, you're coming with me.*>

<*Good.*>

Katrina strode out of her quarters and nodded to Norm and Uma, who both fell in behind her.

"Where are we going, Lady Katrina?" Norm asked.

"To the *Castigation*, then to Nesella Station, where the *Verisimilitude* has docked."

"Cocky fuckers." Uma's low voice was laced with malice. "Always thought they were such hot shit."

"That's cause they are," Norm replied. "Lady Katrina, should I reach out to Korin for your full guard?"

"Not everyone. We need to maintain a presence here on Farsa. But at least a hundred."

"Yes, ma'am."

Katrina considered that she would do well to win over more of the MDF forces on Farsa. They had proven harder to work with than the Adders—the pirates just wanted to be on the winning side and get paid. Many of the MDF personnel believed in law, order. They liked the respect that Lara had garnered for their forces.

Many viewed Katrina as a blight, though currently one that they would have to stomach. So long as the Adders and the MDF were balanced, at least.

Her request for more ships from the other cantons to bolster the MDF would throw off that balance, the implications of which had been weighing on her mind.

It was one of the reasons that she was so eager to get her hands on the *Verisimilitude*. It also meant that she needed to involve the MDF in its capture.

And find something to offer Kruger. Gaining him as an ally in the midst of this would be an important step. One that would be necessary if she did indeed need to move on Lady Marion of Canton Kurgise.

Maybe she could offer Kruger the woman's canton…

First she had to make Malorie less of a burden.

<Demy, the Castigation *is shipping out.*>

<*I know, Captain Jordan has requested that I remain aboard. The new engineering crew is still learning the ropes.*>

<*Good, I'm bringing Malorie, can you get one of those harvester bots up from Revenence Castle before we go?*>

Demy snorted. <*Sorry, Lady Katrina, there's not a snowball's chance in a fusion reactor. I just got wind that they're buried in the back of some storage shed with half a century of other farming equipment. Even if they haven't been crushed under a pile of cultivator spades, it'll take a day or more to get them out.*>

<*Dammit, OK, I guess I'll make do, lugging her braincase around.*>

<*Well…*> Demy began, sounding uncertain about whatever other option she had.

<*Spit it out, Demy.*>

<*On Rockhall, we used these netcrawlers to get parts out of the back ends of the station. We ran them centrally, but they actually supported a local NSAI hookup. I **think** I could hook up Malorie's braincase to one.*>

<*Why the hesitation?*> Katrina asked.

<Well…we got them from a ship that had raided Crossbar awhile back.>

Katrina bit back a harsh response. Not knowing the details of the thousands of surrounding systems was a never-ending pain in the ass, but it wasn't Demy's fault that she had no idea what significance Crossbar held.

Luckily, her silence prompted Demy to fill in the details.

<Right, uh, they're a weird group who got into the whole vampire thing on a planetary scale. We call 'em suckers. Anyway, their general aesthetic is…creepy.>

Katrina glanced down at the case she was carrying, Malorie's brain and life-support systems nestled inside.

<I think creepy suits Malorie. Get one sent over from Rockhall before we depart.>

<I can do you one better, ma'am. There are two in one of the Castigation's bays. Got dumped there when we were pulling the ship out of storage. If memory serves, one has a bad central processor, and the other has some broken legs. Together, I can make something functional.>

Katrina wondered about 'some' broken legs. That, combined with Demy's description of the things as being creepy, piqued her interest.

<Sounds good. I'll pass Malorie off to you once we get aboard.>

<I'll be waiting.>

Katrina closed the connection and considered her next call. This one would be trickier, but it had to happen.

<Colonel Odis, may I have a word?>

<Do I have a choice, Warlord?>

While most of the Adders referred to her as 'Lady Katrina', given her position as the head of the Blackadder canton, the MDF officers preferred to call her 'warlord'. She was certain they meant it as an insult, but she acted as though it were not.

Even if they spoke the word in derision, given the two options, she preferred it. She held no military rank, and appropriating one would not earn her any love from the MDF. Warlord was about as close to a military rank as she would get.

<*I was being polite, Colonel,*> Katrina replied. <*I know things have been tense this past week, but we need to put that behind us as much as we can. While I may have been a catalyst for what happened, I did not instigate this conflict. I did end it, though, and I saved a lot of lives in the process.*>

Katrina spoke the lie with such conviction that she almost believed it herself. Granted. It was not entirely untrue. She *didn't* start this; Admiral Lara was actively working to take whatever the Blackadders had found — namely Katrina herself — by force, if necessary. That precipitated their small conflict on Farsa, which Jace escalated greatly in his bid to take over everything.

<*Very well. What do you want…ma'am?*>

<*We're paying a visit to the Nesella Station to secure the* Verisimilitude. *I want four of your destroyers to accompany us, with enough troops to assault the station if needs be. I'm going to reach out to Admiral Gunter for additional support when we get out there.*>

Colonel Odis laughed. <*You may want to pull in Admiral Leena's ships instead. Gunter is in bed with Kruger. Literally.*>

Katrina's eyes widened at that. <*Good to know, Odis. I may still use Gunter…that is his sector. It would be suspicious if I called in someone else.*>

<*Understood, I think it may be worth devising a way to use Leena, though. Or at least make sure Gunter himself is nowhere near Nesella Station.*>

<*Thanks, Colonel Odis,*> Katrina replied. <*That's very helpful.*>

<*I just don't want to get killed on the mission — looking out for my people, here.*>

That's why I picked you, Odis, Katrina thought. *You're predictable that way.*

<*Excellent. Get your Flight in order and coordinate with Captain Jordan. We're shipping out in thirty minutes.*>

<*We'll be ready,*> Odis replied.

Katrina closed the connection, and then considered the various ways in which taking the *Verisimilitude* could play out.

<*Korin?*> she pinged her head of security. <*You talking with Norm?*>

<*Yeah, we're sorting out who we'll send along with you.*>

A malicious smile crept across Katrina's face. <*Change of plans, keep it to the minimum possible. I want you to do something else while we're away.*>

THE JUMP

STELLAR DATE: 02.03.8512 (Adjusted Gregorian)
LOCATION: *Voyager*, **Monta Station**
REGION: Orbiting Takan, Kashmere System

Troy reviewed the new jump-navigation systems, recalculating their trajectory, triangulating off nearby stars, and confirming with more distant objects.

The dark layer made him nervous. No, not nervous, uncomfortable. It was just so much *nothing*, barring the clumps of dark matter that clustered around stars. Barely detectable, but spelling instant death for any ship that collided with them.

How did they ever manage to map all these jump points out? The time and expenditure must have been significant.

He considered that it probably still was. Dark matter orbited stars just like regular matter. Clear routes between the stars were often in flux, shifting as matter moved about, both in newtonian space, and in the dark layer.

That was part of what made him nervous. The Kashmere System advertised the clear routes to nearby stars, but the safe exit locations were provided by whatever ships had most recently come from those systems. One had to trust that everyone else was operating in good faith.

It was strange to think that—unless one was inside of a federation of some sort—the speed of information between the stars was determined by the routes of freighters, commercial passenger transports, and light courier ships.

All interstellar data flowed through such ships, and some amount of skepticism had to be given to the quality of said data. It could be out of date, wrong, or maliciously altered.

Yet somehow the whole fabric of human commerce and communication seemed to hold together.

Troy wondered if it was just held in place by sheer willpower. After the many interstellar wars of the last five thousand years—the most recent major conflagration only four hundred years in the past— humans and AIs may just want peace badly enough to make it work.

Yeah. Right, Troy laughed to himself. *AIs maybe, humans no.*

Rama leant back in her chair and nodded while reviewing the jump trajectory. "Looks good to me, Troy. You sure you want to dump out of the DL eighty AU out at Midditerra? Gonna be a long flight insystem."

<We want to avoid notice,> Troy replied. <If there is one system in the galaxy that we can't just wander into, this is it.>

"Well, this and Bollam's World."

<Sorry, I thought that went without saying.>

"Look at you, Troy, being all imprecise and making assumptions! I like it." Rama grinned up at her little 'Troy' figurine she'd made. The optics on the *Voyager* were too small to see, and Rama said she hated talking to nothing.

Hence the Troy doll that stood atop the center console.

At first it annoyed Troy—granted, most human particularities did—but he'd grown accustomed to it. He'd also placed a small nano drone on the figurine, so that when Rama talked to it, he could watch as though she were talking to him.

<And look at you, doing the math right on the first try,> Troy replied to Rama. *<Keep that up, and I'll wonder if you've got an NSAI tucked in your head.>*

Rama laughed. She always did whenever he needled her. "Could be, Troy, could be. I got a prybar and squeezed one in."

<Would explain why your head is so misshapen,> Troy shot back.

"Ohhh, look who's talking, Mr. Lumpy Hull."

"Do I have to separate you two?" Carl asked as he climbed up to the cockpit. "Not that I'm sure how we'd do that."

<You could put her in a stasis pod,> Troy suggested.

"Or pull Troy's core," Rama said, grinning widely.

"Fight nice, kids," Carl grunted. "We ready for the jump?"

<Triple-checked,> Troy replied. *<We're in the pocket.>*

Carl chewed on his lip as he looked over the jump calculations. "Stars, this makes me nervous," he muttered.

"Why's that, boss?" Rama asked.

Carl shot her an appraising look. "Because we still haven't worked out the issues with the relays. We just can't get the specs right on the fabbed ones. We need to buy some, but we don't have the right credits."

"I know, Carl, I was messing with you," Rama rolled her eyes. "You and I have only worked together for a bajillion years. You think you'd know how I roll by now."

<It's true, Carl. I understand her humor better than you.>

"Sorry," Carl muttered. "Stress response. Let's just do this, already."

<Approval noted. Initiating jump.>

Troy activated the grav field generators, and an alternating field of positive and negative gravitons flowed out from the *Voyager*, dropping it from normal space into the dark layer.

They were on their way to the Midditerra System.

A NEW OUTLOOK
STELLAR DATE: 02.04.8512 (Adjusted Gregorian)
LOCATION: Katrina's quarters
REGION: Farsa Station, Persia, Midditerra System

Nesella Station lay in orbit of Regula, a smallish ice giant forty-seven AU from Midditerra's star. It was on the same side of the system primary as Persia, making for a somewhat shorter trip, but not much.

Katrina had spent most of the four days researching everything she could about the stations on the outer rim of the Midditerra system. There were thousands of smaller outposts, but only a few dozen major habitats.

Nesella was one of those.

A collection of toroids, it housed over three-hundred-million humans, making it one of the largest population centers in the Midditerra system.

Kruger ruled it in a semi-democratic fashion: democratic in that he held many plebiscites, 'semi' in that he either manipulated the results, or just ignored them.

The man was wily and would make a formidable adversary—which meant Katrina had to ensure he didn't become one.

The single advantage she had over him was that Admiral Lara had ensured that the station masters in the outer system kept limited fleets. She had taxed them heavily and used that money to bolster the MDF.

The end result were stations that needed the MDF for protection and didn't have the resources to extricate themselves from that dependency.

Lara, you were one cunning bitch.

Katrina rose from the desk in the stateroom Jordan had granted her, and stared out at the dark blue orb of Regula. They were four hours from docking at Nesella Station, and she had just exchanged brief pleasantries with Kruger.

Officially, she was visiting him as a matter of state, getting to know the man, and discussing how he would fit into the new government she was organizing.

She suspected he knew the other reason she was coming, though it was hard to know for certain. The *Verisimilitude* was not on record as being docked on the station, and no official logs showed it as having arrived.

It was only through some of Jordan's own contacts that they knew it was there, tucked on the inside of one of the inner rings, out of sight unless you were deep within the station.

The ship's docking location alone spoke volumes.

<Katrina,> Demy's voice came into her mind. *<I believe that I'm ready.>*

*<Is **she**?>* Katrina asked, suppressing a laugh.

She didn't know what form the net crawlers took, she'd not asked for further clarification after Demy's comment referring to them as creepy, but she rather hoped it wasn't too pleasant.

While Katrina wanted Malorie as an ally, she didn't want the woman to think she was absolved of past crimes. Just like she had turned Lord Troan into her creature, she would do the same to Malorie.

<She's complained a lot, but I can tell she likes her new body more than she's willing to admit.>

<How can you tell?>

Demy chuckled. <Her endorphin levels are through the roof.>

<I can't imagine she has the glands to produce many peptides. Unless you added some to control her?>

<I maaaay have done that. But she's triggering their release herself. I'm not doing it to her. She's a masterpiece, though.>

<OK, OK, I get it, you want to show her off, I'm coming.>

<Great, I'll let her know.>

Katrina turned from the window and surveyed her stateroom, ensuring that everything was in order before striding from the room and out into the passageway.

The *Castigation* had started life as a military cruiser, and as such, her stateroom was in officer country. The engineering bays were twenty-two decks down, four-hundred meters aft, and she set off at a brisk pace, moving as quickly as she could while still exhibiting decorum.

She passed a few Adders in the passageways, the pirates moving aside, but none saluting—that was not their way. She did get respectful nods and looks of respect, though.

A few of fear, as well.

That suited Katrina. Loyalty was earned. She'd get there. For now, respect and fear would have to do.

She stopped in the galley to grab an apple, and was still eating it when she arrived in the bay Demy had appropriated for what she joked about as her 'mad scientist experiment'.

"Holy shit," Katrina almost choked on the bite she had just taken of her apple as she saw the thing in the middle of the room.

The first observation she made—other than 'that is one bright red bot'—was that there were a lot of legs.

"Well," Demy said, standing beside what Katrina would now have to think of as Malorie. "What do you think?"

The netcrawler's body was a long, flattened oval that was covered in chitinous scales. It twisted side to side, almost seeming to flow as much as move as it turned to face her.

Attached to the oval were eight long, articulated legs, each with a hook and hasp on the end. They were long, thick, and strong in appearance.

One end of the oval tapered to a point, with several nozzle-like protuberances coming from it. The other end narrowed and angled upward, almost like a long neck, though it had two more appendages on each side.

Arms, Katrina supposed.

Atop the 'neck' was a flattened orb with a red light running its circumference, though there was also a stylized V on one side that Katrina supposed must be the front of the head.

It bobbed up and down, then Malorie's voice emitted from the thing.

"How hideous am I?" she asked, sounding far less certain of herself than Katrina had ever heard before.

Katrina didn't reply as she walked toward Malorie, examining her new body more closely. The main, eight-legged section was nearly two meters long, with the legs stretching out a meter in all directions.

She imagined Malorie's full reach would be over three meters in any direction if she stretched her limbs out. With her limbs mostly folded in—as they were right now—her 'body' was only fifty centimeters or so off the ground. Her neck stretched up nearly a meter, the arm-like appendages on it half a meter long—which put her 'head' at chest height.

"You're not what I expected, that's for sure," Katrina replied as she approached. "Honestly, I was expecting something a bit more...grotesque, considering your warning, Demy.

Demy shrugged. "I could have left her black with some of the strange protuberances that the Crossbar designers had put on, but I figured we don't want to scare people too much. Plus, red is more Malorie's color than black."

"You pick it?" Katrina asked.

"No," Malorie replied. "I did."

"I'll admit, it's a weird crawler design," Katrina said as she trailed a finger along Malorie's neck. "I've never seen one with a head."

"It didn't have one," Demy replied. "It just had a pod-like thing with those four arms. Without the head, she seemed far too insectile. Not to mention she kept bumping into things, with her optics that low."

"Plus my eyes were crotch-height on everyone," Malorie added, rotating her 'head' side to side.

Demy nodded. "And those arms that are now on her neck were angled up from the front of the body. It honestly looked like she was going to disembowel people…or at least grab them in the ass. Anyway, I fabbed up the head and neck bit. It's a little odd looking, but it's slender and flexible, and can fold forward or back, so she can still get into tight spaces if needed."

Katrina laughed. "Demy, I'm not planning on putting her to work in Rockhall. She doesn't need to actually go skittering around on the cargo nets."

"You never know," Demy shrugged. "If you don't like it, we can change her."

"No…please," Malorie said, almost pleading. "I'm just finally getting used to this, let's not go changing me up just yet."

"She had some really bad vertigo at first," Demy explained. "Felt like she was throwing up constantly."

"Which really sucks when you're imagining the whole thing," Malorie added.

"Where's her brain?" Katrina asked. "Down in the body?"

"Yeah," Demy pointed at the forward section. "In there, along with reserve nutrients and backup life-support systems. I left her in the braincase, just used its external connections to link into the crawler's systems. She's still working on coordination, though."

"Standing is hard," Malorie replied. "Walking is almost impossible. So many legs…."

Katrina chuckled. "I didn't expect something quite like this, Malorie. If you don't like it, we can get a bipedal automaton frame for you eventually. I don't know if there are any decent ones to be had in Midditerra, though."

"No!" Malorie almost shouted. "I mean, no...I'm fine."

<I told you she really likes it,> Demy said. <She's playing it off like it's a hardship, but I don't think you could pull her out of that body with a starship.>

<It seems unhealthy,> Sam chimed in. <She shouldn't have such a strong chemical reaction to being in that body.>

<Says the AI that sang with delight at one point after being put into the Castigation,> Demy said with a smirk.

<Well, who doesn't dream of being a warship? After decades in the Havermere, this thing is like a slice of heaven. Granted, I think the body you've given Malorie is an upgrade, but you humans don't. You'll view her as a thing. In my opinion, **that's** what is causing her pleasure.>

<When'd you become such a psychologist, Sam?> Demy asked.

<AIs spend a lot of time studying the particularities of organics,> Sam replied sending the mental equivalent of a shrug. <You're strange, volatile things. I would posit that every AI is a bit of a psychologist.>

Katrina wondered at Sam's words. It made a twisted sort of sense that Malorie would enjoy thinking of herself as a thing. It was how Jace had treated her for years. Katrina suspected the woman viewed herself as contemptible, on some level.

Was letting Malorie embody her own vision of herself a healthy thing? She had no idea. Katrina decided that she didn't care overmuch, either. So long as Malorie was useful, and non-destructive to herself and others, she could inhabit whatever body was available and reasonable.

The one thing she *did* worry about were the hooked claws on those twelve limbs. They looked capable of tearing into a person with little effort.

<Inhibitors?> she asked Demy.

<To the limit. She can't do anything to harm another human. Unless you order her to, of course.>

<Just me?> Katrina asked, arching an eyebrow in Demy's direction.

<Well, and me.> Demy's tone was defensive. <I have to have full access to her systems if I'm to work on her.>

<I suspected. I was just needling you.> Katrina turned back to Malorie. "Well, Malorie, since you're so happy being your creepy bug-self, you can keep it. Not that you have many options. Demy spent too much effort on you to take you back out again. Come along to the bridge, I want you up there while we dock—plus I want to see the crew's reaction."

"I understand," Malorie's voice held a meek note rarely present. "It may take me a bit...like I said, walking is hard."

"What if you pick up four legs and just walk on the other four for now?" Katrina asked.

Malorie lifted her center legs into the air and took a tentative step forward.

"Oh, that is easier!"

"Eventually your brain will be able to operate them all better," Demy said. "Right now, the braincase is trying to simulate a mapping of your brain's ability to control four limbs to twelve. It'll take a bit before it helps build the right neural pathways for more natural control."

"Good, then we'll be on our way. Excellent work, Demy."

"Happy to help," Demy replied with a grin. "Was fun to make something like this. We should try to make Jace into a worm."

Katrina laughed. "That may almost be worth doing. Suitable, at least."

She left the bay and walked slowly down the hall, Malorie skittering along behind her.

"So, Mal, what do you think Kruger's plans are with the *Verisimilitude*?"

Malorie didn't reply, and Katrina turned to see her struggling to get her left foreleg to move at the right time.

"Just a bit harder than I'd thought, give me a moment."

Katrina had to hold back a laugh. Malorie's predicament reminded her of some of the stranger mods she used to see in Luminescent Society when she was younger. Granted, those were all voluntary and often included more organic, or organic-looking, parts of the person's original body.

Malorie finally convinced her front-right leg to lower when she wasn't lifting her rear right, and took a few hesitant steps.

"OK, I think I got this. What were you asking?"

"Kruger, what's his plan, do you think?"

"Hmm..." Malorie tapped one of her upper appendages against her metal head-orb, the *tink tink* sound echoing down the passageway. "That's a good question. The most likely possibility is that he wants to take advantage of any weakness in the MDF to build up his own forces—either by claiming it's necessary for his own protection, or because he thinks he can just do it with impunity."

"That was my top-line assessment, as well. But why the *Verisimilitude*? That's not an easy ship to hide. He'd have to know that I'd want it. Either for the Adders, or for the MDF."

Malorie snorted. Or tried to. The sound was closer to a donkey's bray, and she made an embarrassed gasp afterward. "Demy's a fucking comedian."

"Do you want the body or not?"

"You know, Katrina, you remind me a lot of Jace—and I mean that in the worst way possible."

Katrina was glad that Malorie was behind her—and that her skin was artificial—otherwise the woman would have seen the color drain right out of it.

Doesn't matter. You didn't ask for this. You're doing what you have to, to survive.

"Keep your insight to Kruger," Katrina growled.

"Fine." Malorie didn't speak for a moment, though the *click click click* rhythm of her clawed feet hitting the deck had steadied. "I suppose he might offer it to Marion, or maybe to Gunter. Marion would take it in a heartbeat; she's too stupid to understand the risk that would pose."

"Even after my demonstration down in Selkirk?"

Malorie brayed, but didn't comment on it this time. "Maybe. That may have strengthened her resolve. Like I said, she's not very bright. She has people around her that keep her in check most of the time, though. Doesn't mean that Kruger wouldn't make the offer to her. Mind you, this all assumes that Leon has surrendered the ship to Kruger in some fashion. I have a hard time believing that he'd do that."

"Oh? So what would Leon's play be?"

"Well, did the ship take damage in the fighting?"

Katrina shrugged. "A bit, it got in a dust-up with a pair of MDF cruisers, but it was all extreme range stuff. I can't imagine that the *Verisimilitude* got more than a scratch."

"But it could have," Malorie pressed.

"It could, yeah."

Katrina couldn't imagine Malorie taking a ladder, at least not until she had a handle on using all her legs—in theory, the crawler itself should have no trouble doing it—so she stopped at a lift and waited for the car to come down to their level.

"Well, then, he and Kruger would be working out a deal. But *I* really think that deal would see Leon remain in command of the *'Tude*. He's coveted that position for too long to surrender it mere days after getting his hands on it."

The lift doors opened to reveal a pair of crewmen. One let out a small shriek, while the other swallowed with a worried look on his face.

"You two going to stand in there forever?" Katrina asked. "Also, say hi to Malorie. After her original meat suit got shot up, we had to find her a new body. Like it?"

"Umm...it's fitting," one of the crewmen said, nodding as he slipped past. "Lady Katrina, Lady Malorie."

"Just Malorie," Katrina corrected.

"Er, sorry. Habit."

Katrina walked onto the lift and stood in the corner while Malorie slowly worked her way through the narrow entrance, only getting one leg hooked on the doors.

"Not bad," Katrina said as the doors closed and the lift began to rise.

"Getting the hang of it," Malorie replied. "You'll see me skittering along the overheads in a week, tops."

Katrina snorted. "You're going to scare the shit out of everyone. I think you like the idea."

Malorie's insectile robotic form betrayed no emotion, staying completely still, but her voice held a note of glee. "I just might."

Jordan laughed when Katrina and Malorie entered the bridge, a giggle she tried to stifle that turned into a full-on guffaw.

The rest of the bridge crew wasn't sure how to react, so they kept quiet and tried to pretend they were focused on the final approach to Nesella Station.

"You done, Captain Jordan?" Malorie asked when Jordan finally got herself under control.

The question brought a fresh round of laughter from Jordan, and Katrina rolled her eyes and slapped the captain on the shoulder as she walked past.

"Take it easy, Captain."

"Sure, yeah," Jordan wheezed while the navigator began to chuckle. "It's just…it's just…Mal…you're like a giant lobster. I need to find out if Demy can make big snappy claws for you."

The statement brought a fresh round of laughter from Jordan, and Katrina turned and rolled her eyes. "A bit of decorum? How long 'til we're docked?"

Jordan wiped her eyes while Malorie quietly moved to a far corner.

<*I knew I should have made Demy leave the body black and creepy,*> Malorie said to Katrina.

<*We'll see if we have time for round two later.*>

"We're twenty minutes out," Jordan replied after a moment. "We got an external berth on an outer ring. STC didn't put up a fight when we asked for it. I think they want us as far out on the edge as possible."

Katrina wasn't surprised. The *Castigation* looked like a junk-heap—an appearance the previous stationmaster of Rockhall had deliberately maintained to hide the fact that the vessel was functional. However, what it lacked in looks, it made up for in speed and maneuverability. And weapons. The ship sported more beams than any ship in the Adder fleet, excepting the *Verisimilitude*. It also possessed eight railguns, which was an almost ridiculous number for a ship of its tonnage.

In short, Katrina wouldn't want a ship like the *Castigation* docking at her station, either.

"Smooth otherwise?" Katrina asked

"Well, they told us to shut down our reactors and let a tug bring us in. I told them to suck my ass. They didn't push the issue; I think that Colonel Odis's four

M. D. COOPER

destroyers holding off station helped remind them that we're not some merchant ship popping by with a hold full of cargo."

Katrina nodded as she observed the station and the *Castigation*'s assigned berth. "Our guns won't have a line of sight on anything useful," she said after a moment.

"True, do we need to?" Jordan asked.

"Yes. Take the third berth up from what they offered. Our dorsal rails will have a line of sight on their command deck."

Jordan cast Katrina an appraising look. "You just love to rock the boat, don't you?"

"I've never rocked a boat in my life," Katrina deadpanned.

"Uh...metaphor?"

Katrina winked at Jordan. "I'm messing with you."

"Shit, Katrina, don't do that. You're far too scary to mess with people. Not like lobster lady back there."

<Be a little bit nice to her,> Katrina said privately to Jordan. <I'm trying to make her useful—something she won't be if we all openly mock her.>

Jordan met Katrina's eyes and nodded. <OK, I'll do my best. Hopefully Demy can find some black paint, though!>

Katrina shook her head as Jordan turned and covered her mouth. <Real mature.>

<Sorry!>

"Captain, Lady Katrina," the Adder at the comm station looked up. "The STC has noted our change in vector and they're demanding that we take the berth they assigned."

"Put them on," Katrina said as she strode toward the holotank.

"Aye, ma'am."

A figure appeared in the holotank, a rather tired looking woman, who looked half asleep as she droned on. "...alter vector and proceed to berth seaaaaven aaay daaash niiine onnnne."

"No," Katrina said. "We're taking the berth we're on course for. We expect station to accept our grapple."

"Huh?" the woman looked up and realized she was staring at Katrina. "Oh...uh, who are you?"

"The Warlord," Katrina replied. "I find your assigned berth unacceptable, so I chose a new one."

"You can't—"

"Quiet, woman. I can and I will."

The STC operator glanced to the side and Katrina could tell she was talking to someone else. "But we're not mass balanced for that port," she said hastily.

"Nonsense," Katrina replied. "It's only four hundred meters up on the same ring. You'll hardly need to shift any ballast at all to manage it—or just jack your a-grav. With the troubles, you've only half the normal number of ships docked. You have ample power to do it."

"Umm...I'll have to speak to the stationmaster."

"Good," Katrina nodded. "You do that. We'll be making grapple in three minutes. Nesella Station had better accept."

Katrina didn't wait for the response and killed the comm channel.

"You're so mellow," Jordan said, shaking her head.

Katrina smiled in response. "It's a skill."

Jordan looked to her helm officer. "Let me know if they don't open the clamps in the next minute."

"Aye, ma'am."

Katrina wondered why Jordan seemed unfazed by her demeanor. Nearly everyone else walked on pins and needles around Katrina, but not this woman.

Perhaps it was because she believed she was in Katrina's inner circle—which, if Katrina were honest with herself, was probably true. Katrina had few people she could trust; though she probably *shouldn't* trust Jordan, to be honest.

That's no way to live. I have to put some faith in someone. For now, Jordan, Korin, and Sam will have to do.

"Would you like to come and meet Kruger?" Katrina asked Jordan.

"I've met him before. Boor of a man. I'll pass, unless you think you need me."

Katrina considered it. Jordan would be nice to have around, but she would be more useful on the bridge of her starship. "I could certainly use you, but I think I'd prefer your finger on the trigger out here. Plus, I'll need someone to coordinate with Odis."

"Stars…his parents should have named him Odious. The man takes everything far too seriously."

"Jordan…"

"Yes, Mom, I'll play nice. I assume you're going to take his squad of guards aboard?"

Katrina nodded. "Yes, we'll need all the Adders for Plan B."

"Good ol' Plan B," Jordan said with a shake of her head. "We always fall back to it. Not sure why we don't just start with it."

"First plan always fails," Katrina slapped Jordan on the shoulder. "If we started with B, we'd have to have a C."

Jordan winced and rubbed her shoulder. "Stars your hand is hard, you need to ease up with it. Regarding the plans, we could start with B and then fall back to Plan A—in theory, it's the one with the best outcome."

Katrina laughed. "Now you're just talking crazy talk. OK, I'm off. Wish me luck."

"You don't need luck," Jordan winked. "You're the Warlord."

For some reason, hearing Jordan say it like that made Katrina feel less comfortable, not more.

THE MEET

STELLAR DATE: 02.04.8512 (Adjusted Gregorian)
LOCATION: Outer Ring 19
REGION: Nesella Station, Regula, Midditerra System

To his credit, Kruger met them at the airlock in person.

He was a large man, not bulky, but tall. It reminded Katrina of the Noctus crew of the *Hyperion*, many of whom had been over two and a half meters in height.

"Lady Katrina," he said, extending his hand and not batting an eyelid as her steel-encased fingers grasped his flesh and blood ones.

"It is good to meet you, Stationmaster Kruger. I assume you know why we're here."

Katrina had no desire to beat around the bush. She wanted to feel this man out as soon as possible. Pushing him before he'd felt her out would give her the most honest reactions.

"Because Nesella is the preeminent station in outer Midditerra, and as the new woman in charge, you want to see the best of the best before any other."

Kruger grinned as he said it, seemingly knowing all too well what her intentions were.

So much for catching him off balance.

She eyed the four security personnel behind Kruger and the one flunky standing at his side. There would be more in the crowds on the dock, and there would be automated defenses. The man was no fool.

<Sam, are you making nice with the station AIs?>

<Working on it. There's a few of them, and all but one are heavily sequestered,> the Castigation's AI replied.

<Is that good?>

<No, not really. That one unsequestered AI is in Kruger's head, and is happily keeping the others under its thumb.>

<Interesting,> Katrina replied.

"Well, where shall we go to discuss business, then?" Katrina asked.

"I don't talk shop until I eat," Kruger said with an expansive smile. "You *do* eat with your steel body, right?"

"My skin is metal, not my stomach," Katrina replied coolly.

"Excellent!" Kruger clapped his hands. "Come, one of my favorite restaurants is not far. I have a table waiting for us."

Kruger led them a kilometer down the dock, talking idly about his stations, recent commerce activity, and the problems that the conflict between the Adders and the MDF had caused him.

He dropped that last statement and gave Katrina a significant look to which she smiled and nodded.

"I guess you're grateful that I ended that conflict."

"Did you?" Kruger asked. "Things still seem a bit on edge."

"I said I ended the conflict, I didn't say I waved a magic wand and made everything better."

Kruger cast a sidelong glance at Katrina, then laughed. "Fair enough. Stuff like the rift between the Adders and the MDF doesn't heal overnight. I get it."

A few minutes later, they arrived at the restaurant: a grandiose establishment fronted by a row of marble columns that dominated the concourse running along one of the toroid's spokes.

"Cher Rios," Kruger announced. "One of my favorites."

"Great," Katrina said as she paused, waiting for her guards to enter first and sweep the location. "Looks like my kind of place."

Kruger scowled at her guards as six of them filed past the woman at the podium, ignoring her concerned looks. A minute later, one of them reappeared and nodded to her.

"We're ready," Katrina said to the woman, who glanced at Kruger before nodding and leading them inside.

Malorie—who Katrina had not yet introduced, and whom Kruger had not acknowledged—began to follow them, causing Kruger to finally take notice and glance back at her.

"I'd prefer it if your pet didn't come. Your guards alone are likely to ruin my appetite."

"She's not my pet," Katrina replied. "This is Malorie, formerly the Lady of Revenence Castle. Though chances are that she will be once again."

Kruger's head whipped around, and he paused to look Malorie over.

"Seriously? Malorie?"

"Yeah, stop gawking, haven't you seen a netcrawler bot before?"

Kruger nodded. "Yeah, but not with *your* brain inside of it." He glanced back at Katrina. "Still, are you sure you want her with us? She's so...distasteful."

Katrina reached down and pulled the lightwand from her belt, holding it up in front of Kruger.

"Do you know what this is?"

"A lightwand," he replied.

"Yes," Katrina nodded in agreement. "But not just any lightwand. This is one I took from Lord Wills after he challenged my authority. Soon after, he found its blade inside his head."

Kruger seemed unfazed. "I'd heard of Wills' demise, though I had not picked up on the details. Why are you showing it to me?"

"Just thought I'd remind you of what happened to one of the people who recently defied me."

Kruger snorted and continued walking through the restaurant. "That doesn't surprise me. I've heard you like to throw your weight around. Trust me, though, things are different in the outer system. We're not so easily bullied."

"I suspected as much," Katrina replied as they reached the table. It was near the back of the restaurant, and easily large enough for six people.

Kruger sat first, scowling at Malorie as she positioned herself on one side of the table. Katrina sat last, taking in her surroundings, noting other patrons, and wondering how many of them worked for Kruger.

Given that this restaurant was thirty levels above their intended docking location, the diners were less likely to be his security personnel—though it was possible that he had quickly moved them from one location to another.

"I think you should take me as an object lesson," Malorie said with a rueful laugh. "Although, I think I could probably kill someone in less than ten seconds now, so there are some advantages."

"The outer system stations are the gateway for all of the canton's stolen goods and semi-legal wares," Kruger said, ignoring Malorie. "You need us. And trust me, these stations take a delicate touch. There are a lot of vying interests that have to be carefully juggled."

Katrina imagined that Kruger was right. Even his smallest stations had populations in the millions. Nesella alone vied with some of the cantons in population and power.

Add to that all of the disparate parties who did business in the stations, and you had a recipe for disaster waiting around every corner.

"You do admirable work, I'm sure," Katrina replied. "My visit is to assure you that the MDF will continue to keep the outer system safe. I've demonstrated this by bringing along four destroyers with teams of crack troops aboard."

"Colonel Odis's soldiers, I assume you mean," Kruger nodded. "I couldn't help but notice them lingering out there as you docked. I also couldn't help but notice how your rusty old ship's weapons have my command deck in their sights."

Katrina smiled and inclined her head. "I'm glad you're so observant. My people take my safety very seriously."

<Any progress, Sam?> she asked as Kruger began to speak about his security troubles on the stations, and why he had begun to consider increasing the strength and authority of his police forces.

<I may have a way to let the dogs slip their leashes, but I'll probably only get one shot. So I'd rather not test it until the time comes.>

<OK, but what's the likelihood of success? Am I going to be flapping in the wind here?>

Sam laughed. <That's a funny visual. Let's just say you'd better make sure there are no autoturrets in line of sight before we make a move.>

<And Norm?>

<Nearly in position.>

Katrina turned her attention back to Kruger, who was going on about some problems he had with representatives from different cantons getting into fights.

His tirade was interrupted when a waitress came and asked what they'd like to drink.

"An iced tea," Katrina said, while Kruger ordered a red wine.

"No alcohol?" he asked.

"I don't find that I have a taste for it anymore," Katrina replied. "Most food is a bit bland, but tea seems to still register pleasantly."

"I suppose I can see how that would be the case," Kruger nodded. "I assume that your skin replacement was not an entirely voluntary event."

"Well," Katrina glanced at Malorie. "Mal here had me whipped until my skin was hanging from my body in strips. Then some folks tried to kill me, making it even worse. The time to properly heal wasn't available, so I opted to go for this epidermis instead."

Kruger whistled and looked Malorie up and down. "And so this is your punishment, Malorie?"

Malorie raised her four arms in a strange shrug. "More like this is what Katrina's version of saving my life looks like."

Kruger leant back in his chair and stroked his chin. "Interesting. Yet you seem loyal to her."

" 'Loyal' is a strong word. 'Beholden' may be closer."

Kruger turned back to Katrina. "I must say, there's more to you than meets the eye. I thought you were just an opportunistic bitch. Right place, right time and all that. But something else is afoot with you."

"As it is with you," Katrina replied. "Not a lot of people around here with an AI as sophisticated as yours inside their heads. Jasper, I believe his name is?"

Kruger's eyes narrowed. "You are devious. Jasper does not advertise himself."

"You also have something that belongs to me on your station," Katrina pushed harder. She wanted to see what this man did when his back was against the wall verbally before she put it there physically.

"There are a lot of things on this station that belong to you." Kruger took the glass of wine that the waitress handed him, and swirled it gently, breathing in the aroma, closing his eyes as he did so. "Your canton has over one hundred stores here, as well as a shipyard. The Adders practically own a dozen bars, given the amount of credit they spend at them. Which are you referring to?"

<Norm's ready. Odis's ships are in position,> Jordan said, her voice a quiet whisper in Katrina's mind.

"The *Verisimilitude*," Katrina replied, silently reveling in the perfect timing of Jordan's message.

Kruger didn't reply, instead he turned to his right and smiled at a man who was approaching.

"Admiral Gunter!" Kruger rose, smiling broadly. "How nice of you to join us."

Katrina rose as well and offered her hand to Gunter. "Admiral. I wasn't aware you were on the station. When I inquired, your aides told me you were at Teegarten."

Gunter shook Katrina's hand, and took a seat midway between her and Kruger. "Must have been a miscommunication. I've been inspecting the garrison here. Making certain it is ready for what may come."

"Are you expecting something?" Katrina asked.

"The MDF is always expecting something," Gunter replied evenly.

Katrina was dismayed at the man's attitude. He didn't like her—that much was obvious—but he also didn't possess the subtlety to hide it from her.

"Good," Katrina replied. "I agree that we'll be needing the MDF to defend Midditerra very soon. I—"

"Lady Katrina," Gunter interrupted her. "I must ask. Where is Admiral Lara? The official dispatches say that she has been arrested and detained for crimes against the cantons. The Council has also released statements in support of this, but theirs were considerably delayed."

"That's true," Katrina replied. "The Council takes some time to convene and agree on anything. However, we had a successful meeting. They are even going to send ships to the MDF to bolster its forces."

"This is all highly irregular," Gunter shook his head. "There should be a tribunal—"

"Admiral Gunter," Katrina interjected. "I'm not sure how you have missed this, but that is not how things work here in the Midditerra System. We pay lip service to civilization at best. Why, not a week ago, I was a slave working for Malorie here," Katrina gestured at Malorie's red robotic form, "being beaten if I didn't meet my sithri quota. I was captured in the Bollam's World system by Jace and the *Verisimilitude*..."

Katrina's voice broke for a moment as her thoughts turned to Juasa, and she drew in a slow breath, grinding her teeth before continuing.

"So don't speak to me of due process and honor. This is a star system of thieves and pirates. You're all complicit in slave trading, acts of larceny on a stellar scale, and a host of other horrid crimes. I'm just a mirror for what you really are."

Gunter paled as she spoke, and his lips drew into a thin line. Kruger, on the other hand, began to smile wider the more she spoke.

After a brief pause, the stationmaster clapped and let out a cry of delight. "Finally! Someone who calls a spade a spade. Warlord Katrina, you are a delight to both my eyes and my ears."

"In light of that, Stationmaster Kruger, tell me about the *Verisimilitude*."

"Oh ho!" Kruger raised his hands and smiled. "We're just getting started with the foreplay. Let's not rush to the main event so quickly."

Katrina was finished with foreplay. It was time for the main event.

<Jordan, Sam. Do it.>

ADDERS
STELLAR DATE: 02.04.8512 (Adjusted Gregorian)
LOCATION: Lady Marion's mansion
REGION: Canton Kurgise, Persia, Midditerra System

Korin crouched behind a boulder in the deepening night, looking out over the manicured lawns surrounding Lady Marion's estate, deep in the heart of Canton Kurgise.

His assault force—thanks to some advanced drones provided by the Warlord—had bypassed Marion's first layer of security, blinding her cameras and sensors to the assault team's approach.

Though Korin knew Katrina had significantly more advanced technology, the approach had been harrowing. The knowledge that the tech *should* work, and trusting one's life to said tech, were entirely different things.

Once in position, the teams only had to wait until the prescribed hour—which was now upon them. If no stand down order was received in the next minute, they would proceed with the breach.

To either side of Korin were his best Adders. Veterans of the recent fight against the MDF, and Jace's loyalists. Many of them were from the group that sided with Katrina at Rockhall, and others were men and woman from Revenence Castle that he trusted with his life.

They held their rifles ready, a motley collection of ballistic and kinetic weapons, along with a few beam rifles. The latter in the hands of trusted crack shots.

Whenever Korin thought about it too much, he couldn't help but wonder about Katrina's trust in him. He had no experience organizing an assault like this. No experience leading a coordinated group.

Still, she had reviewed his plan and agreed that it was the best one they had. She had offered an MDF gunnery sergeant to help with the coordination, but Korin knew his Adders weren't yet ready to fight alongside the MDF on the field.

In the end, they were irregulars fighting against another force of irregulars. They'd win the way the Adders always won—through determination and grit.

With any luck, the element of surprise would be enough to set the Kurgise guards back and win the day. Once Lady Marion was in their hands, the order would be given for Canton Kurgise's ships to stand down, and that would be that.

He resisted the urge to let out a rueful laugh—things could also devolve further. Things going to hell in a handbasket was always an option.

The first targets were the bunkers set into the long, sloping lawn that surrounded the mansion. Narrow slits were visible, and within, guards were waiting to be slaughtered.

Korin watched as the timer on his armor's HUD counted down to zero, then waited for the first shots. No signal to attack was needed—no one wanted a burst of EM to let the enemy know something was up.

A moment later, rail-fired rounds streaked out of the trees, hitting the bunkers set into the lawn, the concussive blasts breaking through the protective shields and showering the interior with hot shrapnel.

Without waiting to see the results of the rail shots, HE rounds were fired into the bunkers, hopefully taking out any who survived the initial salvo.

Korin and his squad rushed from the trees, screaming as they raced across the neatly trimmed grass, trusting in the Adders on the rail guns to take out the gun emplacements further up the lawn.

Weapons fire streaked down from the Kurgise mansion, and return fire lanced out from the tree line, hitting guards and weapons emplacements, taking them down one by one.

A series of rounds streaked by Korin's head, and he dropped near one of the bunkers, trying to tell where the shooter was located. Two of his squadmates fell prone with him, peering over the bunker's low rise, when a round was fired out through the bunker's narrow viewing slit, catching an Adder in the chest and flinging him backward.

Korin swore and rolled aside, firing wildly into the bunker before remembering his HE grenades and tossing one in.

"Fire in the hole!" he screamed, rising and running from the bunker.

A second later, the grenade exploded, and flames shot out from the firing slit. He looked around and saw that two members of his squad were down, and the other nine were laying prone as weapons fire rained down from the Kurgise mansion.

"C'mon, you lazy assholes, this place isn't going to surrender to cowards!"

It wasn't his best line, but as Korin turned and raced up the lawn, his HUD showed the whole squad rising and following after him.

Despite the brave face he put on, fear clutched at Korin's chest, and each breath felt like it might be his last. Somehow he managed to push down the fear and focus on the task ahead of him: make it to the balustrade at the edge of the mansion's garden. If they could make it there, they could circle around to the south and take out the heavy gun he could see tearing into the Adders moving up the lawn.

Movement to his right caught Korin's attention, and he saw Gerry draw even with him as they sprinted up the slope. Then a rail shot from the mansion fired, and a white-hot streak tore the Adder in half, spraying blood and gore across the lawn.

I played cards with Gerry last night. We bet on what vid we'd watch when this was over....

Korin pushed the thoughts from his mind.

The balustrade. Reach the balustrade.

A moment later he was there, crashing into it and dropping prone as rail shots slammed into the other side. The balustrade was a waist-high wall meant to provide protection to the mansion's defenders. An added bonus for the Adders was that its strength meant it could hold back significant weapons fire.

At least for a little while.

Seven other members of his squad reached the balustrade's temporary safety a moment later. All that was left of the twelve who had set out from the forest's edge less than a minute before.

"Korin!" one of the Adders wailed. "This is suicide! We can't take the mansion!"

"We *have* to," Korin screamed back as another heavy rail shot streaked overhead, this one drawing a line into the woods where an explosion marked the end of one of the Adder's crew-served railguns.

Katrina...if you sent us here to die....

<Move all firing positions!> Korin cried out. The Adders were supposed to have already done that, but some seemed slow on the uptake.

A shot from the woods lanced across the lawns and hit the large railgun, where it sat atop a low tower on the house's southern corner. A grav shield flared around the tower, and the Adder rail shot was deflected, sparks showering down across the lawn.

"We gotta take that gun out!" Korin screamed and began to move alongside the low wall. He rounded a corner and saw four Kurgise soldiers approaching.

Both groups froze for a moment, until Korin remembered his grenades once more. He tossed one and ducked back around the corner, relief flooding him as a body flew over the balustrade in the wake of the explosion.

He slid around the corner, firing wildly on the enemy's position, only to find that they were all dead.

"Easy now, Korin," one of the Adders on his squad laughed as they advanced past him.

Korin reloaded his rifle. "Yeah, that's right, you go in the front, then, if you're so hot to trot."

The speaker—Cami, he realized now—gave him a rude gesture and led the way along the wall until they reached another corner. She unhooked a grenade from her belt and lobbed it over the wall, flattening herself as the explosion sprayed dirt and debris in the air.

Korin noted that the Adder rail fire from within the tree line had ceased. He didn't blame them. No one wanted to make themselves a target. Luckily, it seemed that his squad was beyond the firing angles for the railgun in the southern tower.

"Let's move," he ordered, and peeked up over the wall, sweeping his rifle across the garden, while Cami leant around the wall to ensure there were no live enemies waiting.

Both areas were clear, and the Adders rushed across the patio to the mansion. Korin watched another team a hundred meters to the west also reach the house, and gave them a thumbs-up.

Cami had shot out a window and was firing on something inside the mansion while Korin moved closer to the tower housing the railgun. It appeared to be on the third floor, and he gestured for his squad to follow him to the ground floor window.

Sure enough, it was unshielded, and he broke the plas and tossed a flashbang inside.

He crouched back against the wall and saw Cami, still shooting into the mansion.

<Cami, get over here!>

<There are four of them, I can't cross in front of this window without getting my ass shot off!>

"Shit!" Korin swore. He glanced at the other six members of the squad and gestured at the window behind him. "Secure the ground floor of the tower, we'll be back in a moment."

He didn't wait to see if they'd followed his orders before moving back toward Cami's position.

Kinetic rounds sprayed out of the window, creating a no-man's-land of deadly weapons fire that Cami's armor could not hope to deflect.

Korin grabbed the last HE grenade off his belt and held it up, gesturing for Cami to do the same. She nodded, grabbed a grenade, and he signaled a three count before they both tossed their grenades through the window.

The flames hadn't finished pouring out of the window before Cami was racing toward Korin, screaming as she ran.

"Nice battle cry," Korin said with a laugh as she whipped past him toward the window at the base of the tower.

The rest of the team had already disappeared inside, and she stopped next to it and glanced back at Korin. "I know, I scream like a man. It's demeaning."

"Har har."

She looked inside the window and appeared satisfied with what she saw, jumping through a moment later. Korin followed without checking and found himself next to Cami in a darkened room with two dead Kurgise guards on the floor, the bodies surrounded by his squad.

"You all circle-jerking over them, or something?" he asked while pointing at the stairs. "Let's get up there. Those asshats are tearing our people apart."

The *kachug kachug* of the railgun thundered above them, and Korin led the charge up the circular staircase, firing wildly as soon as he reached the second floor—which was empty, save for racks of tungsten rounds.

Before going up the last staircase, he grabbed his final flashbang and tossed it up, rushing up the stairs a second later.

When he reached the third floor, he found two stunned men and the railgun. One got a bullet in the head from him, and Cami put down the other.

<Southern gun is down,> he announced. <*I repeat, the southern gun is down.*>

Now they just had to find that bitch, Lady Marion.

TURNOVER

STELLAR DATE: 02.04.8512 (Adjusted Gregorian)
LOCATION: Inner Ring 11
REGION: Nesella Station, Regula, Midditerra System

"I need backup, Odis, you flaming dink. *Today*," Norm called out over the audible comms. "We're pinned down, taking heavy fire."

<*So are we, you pirate moron. We're making progress. The more pressure we put on them here, the less you'll get down there.*>

A pulse grenade sailed through the air and landed on the dock next to Norm. He dove behind a crate a second before it went off, and let out a string of curses that even he almost blanched at.

"Well, I don't think they got the memo!"

Norm peered over the crates at the two entrances to the *Verisimilitude*. One opened up into its larger cargo bay, and another, on a gantry above, opened up into its crew decks.

Both were filled with the ship's crew, firing down on the Adders below.

So much for brothers and sisters in arms, Norm thought as he fired a round into the lower bay while moving into better cover.

They were all Adders, but the *'Tude's* crew didn't seem to care—not that many of Jace's loyalists did. He supposed it didn't matter. His team's job was to keep the ship's crew busy, and ensure no station security came to provide backup, while Odis's team did their part.

Even though the directive for Odis to take the ship had come from Katrina, it rankled that it was not Adders boarding the vessel. A part of him worried that once the MDF had their hands on it, they wouldn't want to give it back.

Of course, they all—Adders and MDF alike—answered to the Warlord, and Norm was certain she'd have her way. Though he'd only known her a few days, he was certain that Katrina was not a woman one would cross. At least not more than once.

Norm had moved into a new position and was firing into the open doors when he saw one of his teams advancing toward the lower entrance and waved them back.

"Sherry, what the hell are you doing?"

"I just saw some of them pull back further inside," she replied, leapfrogging her team forward.

"Yeah, but—shit! Behind you!"

Six station security guards had just rounded a corner behind Sherry's position, rifles leveled. Norm rose and fired at them, driving them back, but not before Sherry took a pulse shot to the head.

He watched her drop like a sack of rocks, and hoped she was just stunned...the station guards were not known for keeping their rifles on low-powered settings.

"Stand down!" Norm called out. "We're here on the Warlord's business."

Two of the station security guards took a step back, but another raised his rifle and fired a shot at another member of Sherry's team.

"Fuck!" Norm swore.

He wasn't going to dick around with the security asshats any more than he had to. He lobbed a conc grenade at them and got ready to shoot at anyone who didn't bugger off.

* * * * *

Kruger swore, and Gunter glanced at him in alarm. She noticed that the other diners in the restaurant were giving them cautious looks. Not the looks she'd expect to see from bystanders witnessing an argument, but rather the cautious glances of people waiting for the signal to move.

"What are you doing, Katrina?" Kruger said, shaking his head. "That ship is under my protection!"

"And you're under mine," Katrina replied to Kruger, before turning to look at Gunter. "Not his. Gunter can't give you the *Verisimilitude*, and you can't claim it for yourself. The ship is mine."

"You don't need to do this," Gunter said to Katrina. She couldn't tell if he was worried for himself, or worried that Katrina had made a terrible blunder.

Given that he had hidden the fact he was on the station, she could come to no other conclusion than that he was acting duplicitously.

"Who does Leon answer to?" Katrina asked. "You, Admiral, or you, Stationmaster? Tell him to stand down."

<I have liberated the AI who controls the docking systems, Pishma. She has overridden the docking clamp releases for the Verisimilitude. It won't be going anywhere.>

<Good work, Sam,> Katrina replied. <Does she have control over station security or section lockdown systems?>

<No, that's Barry. We're working on him, he's…unwell.>

Katrina sighed as she regarded the two men before her. <Don't let me distract you, then.>

"Leon's deal is with me," Kruger said after a moment. "He traded me the ship for a healthy sum—though the transaction hasn't been completed yet."

"And how did you think that I wouldn't notice you flying around with my ship?" Katrina asked.

Kruger laughed softly. "Well, in all honesty, I didn't expect you to last this long—or to learn of its presence this quickly. Congratulations."

"What was your part in this, Gunter?" Katrina asked, turning to the Admiral. "Were you offering Kruger security while he made his play?"

"It's mutual," Gunter ground out the words. "No way a canton is running Midditerra—especially not some slave from Malorie's sithri fields. The *Verisimilitude* is payment to Kruger for his support and financial contribution in overthrowing you. I *was* planning on bringing in my fleet to kick you off Farsa Station, but you've made things a lot easier. Thanks for that."

Katrina shrugged. "Just trying to help. Out of curiosity, which of the cantons was going to take the lead in supporting you for my job?"

Gunter's lips drew a thin line across his face.

"It wasn't…Marion of Kurgise, by any chance, was it?" Katrina asked with a cruel laugh. "I mean, it's not Wills or Troan, that's for sure. Armis is too principled. But Marion would be just right. Not too much to lose, a lot to gain; plus, she's fucking Kruger, just like you, Gunter."

She had suspected that Gunter didn't know that particular detail, and his widening eyes confirmed it.

"Why, you little rat," Gunter said, glaring at Kruger.

Kruger only shrugged. "I like added insurance."

Gunter rose from his chair and pointed at Katrina. "Arrest—" he began to say, then his words cut off. He tried to speak, but failed, eyes bulging as he glared at Katrina.

All around them, the other diners rose. From what she could see in Gunter's mind, half worked for him, and the other half for Kruger. There was only one couple in a far corner that was actually present for the dining experience.

Naturally, they looked terrified.

Katrina saw that Kruger tried to keep a cold look on his face, but it was wavering as Gunter struggled to speak.

"Draw your sidearm," Katrina ordered the Admiral.

Without hesitation, Gunter followed her directions.

"Put the barrel in your mouth."

Gunter complied, and Kruger's face drained of all color.

"Stationmaster Kruger," Katrina turned to the man. "Tell your people to stand down. If you don't, Malorie will tear your head off."

"I've been itching to kill someone with this body," Malorie whispered, edging closer to Kruger.

Kruger opened his mouth to speak, but then stopped. He gasped, trying to get a word out, but was only able to grunt.

"What are you doing?" Malorie asked, swiveling her head toward Katrina. "Let Kruger speak before his flunkies kill us."

"I'm not doing that to him," Katrina said, looking around at the confused undercover MDF soldiers and perplexed station personnel. None had drawn their weapons yet, though more than a few hands were resting on pistol grips.

"Everyone stand down," Katrina called out. "If you don't, these two fools both die. My ships have key sections of the station in their sights, and we've taken the *Verisimilitude*."

<We've not,> Sam interrupted.

<I know that, Sam. What I really care about is whether or not Kruger's AI is doing this to him?>

<Maybe? I have a suspicion that his AI is actually the one that runs everything around here.>

Katrina stretched a foot under the table and touched her ankle to Kruger's thigh, passing a large dose of nano into his body.

He winced as she did it and then a moment later went limp, his head hitting the table.

The shock of seeing Kruger drop pushed the onlookers over the edge, and she could see that the room was hers.

"Stand down *now!*" Katrina cried out as she rose, glaring at the guards and soldiers around her. "I want everyone's guns on the floor."

As she issued the order, the MDF soldiers that had waited outside the restaurant rushed in, adding additional enforcement to her order. The station guards and MDF soldiers slowly complied, and Odis's troops began to round them up.

Katrina glanced at Gunter and nodded at the man, releasing her control over him.

"It's done. More importantly, you're done."

His eyes were wide as he pulled the gun partway out of his mouth, staring at Katrina with undisguised fear.

Then he pulled the trigger.

CAPTURING MARION
STELLAR DATE: 02.04.8512 (Adjusted Gregorian)
LOCATION: Lady Marion's mansion
REGION: Canton Kurgise, Persia, Midditerra System

Korin raced through the mansion, coordinating with the other Adders who had breached the building. Some focused on taking out the remaining defensive emplacements, while others focused on the hunt for Lady Marion.

"Cami!" he called out. "Take Bart and Friz and check down that hall. Rumsey and I are going to check out the top floor."

"You got it, Boss," Cami called back, and disappeared around the corner, following the route to what his map referred to as the 'family chambers'.

He was split on what Lady Marion would likely do. She seemed like the 'run away' sort. The question was, would she run to her bedroom, like the fool she often seemed to be, or attempt an actual escape?

There was a shuttle on the roof, and the scan feeding down from the ships above showed that it was still in place. If he were fleeing a sinking ship, that's the route he'd take.

Rumsey was in the lead, and checked around a corner before signaling to Korin that the coast was clear. They rushed down a passage, and then turned into a staircase.

"Hate stairs," Rumsey grunted.

"Wanna take a lift?" Korin asked with a laugh.

"Fuck no."

They hugged the outside wall, Rumsey's gun trained on the landing above, while Korin kept his aimed at the doorway they'd just come through.

A second later, a figure appeared, and he almost fired until he realized it was Cami.

"The fuck, woman!" Korin whispered over comms. "Don't *do* that to me."

"Bob's team has that wing covered, I figured you'd probably need me to save your ass again."

"I distinctly recall saving your ass last time," Korin shot back.

Bart and Friz—all that remained of the initial twelve in his squad—followed Cami into the stairwell, and they continued to work their way up, passing the first landing, and then the second, finally stopping at the third.

Knowing that half his squad was now dead or injured on this cursed mansion's grounds angered Korin in a way he hadn't felt before. That Katrina could send him on this mission in such a rush...she had to know he'd suffer losses like this.

"And toooooop floor," Friz announced, his frequently ill-timed humor still in place despite the night's events. "Please watch your step getting off the li—"

A shot came through the door and ricocheted off Friz's armor.

"Smooth move," Cami said, and dove to the other side of the doorway at the top of the stairs, firing out into the hall beyond.

"I was just drawing them out," Friz retorted.

Cami laid down more fire, while Korin and Rumsey got ready to dash to cover on the far side of the hall.

When Cami paused to reload, they made their break, reaching the far side of the hall and stacking up behind a column.

Cami fired again, but no return shots came, and Korin peered around the column to see three Canton Kurgise soldiers, dead in the corridor.

"Sad little fuckers," Cami said as she strolled out from behind her cover.

A shot rang out and hit Cami in the right leg, tearing it clear off her body. Korin saw the shooter, and let fly with a barrage of bullets, taking the enemy out as he rushed down the corridor.

Korin reached the end of the passage, where he confirmed that *now* the Kurgise shooters were all down before turning back to see Rumsey bent over Cami.

"Go, you idiots!" Cami called out. "My armor's sealing it up."

"Stay with her," Korin ordered Rumsey as Bart and Friz rushed down the hall toward him.

He checked around the corner once more, and then the three Adders moved toward the doors at the end of the hall that led to the landing pad.

Korin cracked one open and peered out to see two Kurgise guards escorting Lady Marion to the shuttle. He didn't hesitate and fired a shot into the back of one of the enemies.

The man didn't fall, but spun to see three Adders with weapons trained on him.

"Guns on the ground!" Korin screamed.

"Shoot them!" Marion yelled, but one of the guards was already dropping his rifle. The other followed a second later.

Korin walked toward Lady Marion, a grin on his face. "Well my lady, it seems as though the Adders have bested Kurgise yet again."

Maybe this was worth it. It better have been.

"Pirate scum," Marion spat. "The council is going to destroy your new canton leader!"

"Right," Korin snorted. "I'm on pins and needles."

"Stand down!" a voice thundered through the air, and bright lights shone down on Korin and the rooftop landing pad.

He looked up to see a shuttle, accompanied by a dozen fighters, slowing to a stop over the Kurgise mansion.

The voice from above came again. "By the order of Lady Armis, stand down. Lady Marion has claimed sanctuary with Draus, and we will see it given."

Friz lowered his rifle and glanced at Korin. "Fuckin' Draus, always ruining the party."

SANCTUARY
STELLAR DATE: 02.04.8512 (Adjusted Gregorian)
LOCATION: Lady Marion's mansion
REGION: Canton Kurgise, Persia, Midditerra System

Armis stepped out of the shuttle and walked toward Marion, who stood smirking at the Adder pirates.

Stupid woman…you were seconds away from capture and stars knows what else.

"Marion, come with me." Armis grabbed the leader of Canton Kurgise's arm. "We must go."

Marion turned on Armis, her golden eyes gleaming in the night. "Leave? But you're here. I've claimed sanctuary."

"To gain sanctuary, you have to come to my canton," Armis said, refraining from berating Marion for not knowing council law.

"We wanted you alive, Marion," one of the Adders said, his voice a low growl. "But whether you're dead or alive, Kurgise is ours now. Adder and MDF ships are surrounding Kurgise stations and strongholds as we speak."

"No!" Marion shouted, spinning to face Armis. "Is that true?"

Armis nodded. "It was a coordinated assault that started minutes after the attack here. It was only through dumb luck that I was nearby and able to answer your call for sanctuary."

"That metal bitch!" Marion shrieked. "She can't *do* this. She—"

"Marion, shut up," Armis ordered. "Get on the shuttle. You can't solve anything, standing on your roof and raving like a crazy woman."

Marion's mouth hung open for a moment before snapping shut. She shot the Blackadder pirates one final cold look, and stormed past Armis toward the shuttle. Armis gave the two pirates a final look, as well.

Although...they aren't really pirates.

From what her HUD told her, both of the men on the rooftop were native to Persia. They'd been born on this planet, lived hard—dare she even say, miserable—lives until they found a place in the Blackadder.

Armis still remembered when it had been Revenence Canton—technically, it still was. But once Jace took over, he had insisted that it simply be called 'the Blackadder'.

They were well rid of that scum, though, even if it seemed that Katrina was worse.

"Remember," she called out to the two men. "The survivors are prisoners of war. You may not sell them as slaves or treat them unfairly until the council has met to review this matter."

"Go on then." The man who had spoken before waved her off. "Take the Lady of Nothing and get gone."

Armis sighed and turned, walking toward her shuttle. The whole way, her back felt itchy, and she wanted to run, but knew she had to maintain her decorum.

Making a habit of this.

She had to trust that the pirates wouldn't shoot, not with her fighters hovering overhead.

Of course, she'd be a fool to assume that there were no heavy weapons aimed at her ships. For the Adders to take the mansion in a matter of minutes, they would have rails or more in the surrounding forest.

That they had managed to get this close before launching the assault meant only one thing: Katrina's tech was in play, here.

Armis made it to shuttle unscathed, and met Marion's eyes.

"You could take them," the unseated canton leader said. "They only have a half-dozen rail emplacements in the woods."

"And they have a cruiser overhead," Armis added. "No, I don't think I'll go down in a blaze of glory with you. I would prefer you to shut up and let me think. We have to do something about Katrina fast. She's getting out of hand."

"Well, yes, that much is obvious. You have—"

"Marion," Armis said putting a hand to her forehead. "What part of 'shut up' don't you understand?"

Marion shot her a cold look but didn't speak further, as the shuttle lifted off and climbed through the skies until it reached its cruising altitude.

"We're out of range of their ground weapons," the shuttle pilot called back.

Armis didn't think that the Adders would have shot at a Draus shuttle. That being said, it was nice to be far, far away from their guns.

They passed over the Revenence Estate, and then the western coast of the continent. Armis felt relief wash over her as the dark surface of the ocean filled the horizon.

There were many powers on Persia, and in the Midditerra system at large, but one thing had been true for generations.

Draus controlled the sea.

Not only that, but her submarine drones were able to provide direct protection for her shuttle.

With her level of worry suitably diminished, Armis looked again at Marion—who was quietly fuming—and asked, "What did you do?"

"Me?" Marion asked, outrage clear in her tone of voice. "Why do you think that *I* did something? We've seen what Katrina can do, she doesn't need provocation."

"She also doesn't need the added distraction of governing *everything* herself. She's making examples and taking out the defiant. You're not worth making an example of—not after what she did to Troan and Wills."

"Gee, thanks, Armis. You're such a delight."

Armis shrugged. "I'm trying to keep this star system from tearing itself apart. Now. What did you do?"

"Accuse all you want." Marion folded her arms across her chest. "*I* didn't do anything."

"OK, thanks for equivocating. So one of your allies did something. Who was it? Urdant? Illyra? Kruger?"

Marion's eyes widened a millimeter, and Armis knew she'd found the one.

Kruger.

"Ever the profiteer." Armis shook her head. "Did he steal a bauble for you that Katrina will want?"

"Not for me, directly," Marion equivocated. "But it will help, that's for sure."

"Spit it out, already."

"He worked out a deal to take ownership of the *Verisimilitude*."

"From…who is the first mate on that ship…Leon?" Armis asked after looking it up. She'd kept extensive records of every Blackadder ship—as much as she was able to, at least. Jace had never run a particularly organized establishment.

"Yeah." Marion nodded, a wicked smile on her lips. "Kruger is going to use it and some merchant ships to bolster the outer system defenses, while Admiral Gunter takes a force insystem and captures Farsa."

"That would be fantastic. If Katrina were on Farsa."

Armis let the words fall and watched as a look of confusion came over Marion.

"Where is she?"

"Last I heard, on her way to Nesella station. I suppose this explains why."

"Shit!" Marion swore. "She'll ruin *everything*."

"That's been her modus operandi for the past week and a half. Why change now?"

"Still, maybe Gunter will be able to take her out while she's in the outer system."

Armis nodded. It was possible. Of course, that would put Admiral Gunter in control of the MDF. He was certainly preferable to Katrina, but not her first choice by a long shot.

"Well, we know one thing, at least," Armis said, giving Marion a level stare.

"What is that?"

"Katrina wasn't afraid to wipe you out for supposed collaboration with Kruger, who may or may not have even been actively working against her. She's even more ruthless than I thought."

"Bitch," Marion muttered again. "We have to stop her."

Armis agreed. They did, and she was starting to form an idea as to how they'd pull it off.

ONE SMALL JUMP

STELLAR DATE: 02.05.8512 (Adjusted Gregorian)
LOCATION: BWSS *Nova Star*
REGION: Interstellar space near the Midditerra System

"All fleet elements are assembled and in jump formation, Admiral Pierson," the Fleet Coordination Officer announced from his station on the *Nova Star*'s bridge.

"Very good, Lieutenant," Pierson replied with a small nod. "Instruct all ships to proceed with the jump."

"Yes, Admiral," The FCO replied, and bent to his task. Though the coordination officer ensured all the ships had received Pierson's orders, it was really the fleet NSAI that ensured the ships were on the correct vectors and ready to jump.

This final leg of the journey would take just one day, and when they arrived on the edge of the Midditerra system, they would strike hard and fast at the outer defenses, then move insystem. Their ultimate destination would be determined by intel they'd get after their arrival, but Pierson's money was on Farsa Station.

That's where power was held in Midditerra. If not there, then it would be on Persia, the planet below.

The leading elements of the Bollam's World fleet, under the command of Admiral Dalia, began to transition into the dark layer: a division of destroyers and light cruisers that would take out any defenses and kick off long-range kill shots aimed at known stationary defenses in the system.

Though the division was small—only four hundred and thirty destroyers, and seventy-four light cruisers—it would be more than enough to secure a beachhead for the rest of the fleet.

The rest of the fleet was moving at a slower velocity, and though they would jump in just a few minutes, they would not arrive until more than twelve hours later.

By then, Admiral Dalia should have current intel that would guide their next actions.

It was a risky play; Pierson could be jumping the bulk of the fleet into a trap. But he had faith in Dalia that either she would clear the way, or get a warning to him if things went terribly wrong.

Even if that was the case, he was hopeful that the delay in the two-prong assault would make MDF buy Dalia's feint, and give him an advantage he could exploit.

Only time would tell.

Attempting to take a star system with only four thousand ships was an incredible gamble. Then again, the BWSF wasn't worried about taking and holding the Midditerra System. They just wanted the Streamer Woman and her ship.

She'd better be there, or a lot of us are going to die for nothing, Pierson thought as the last of Dalia's ships disappeared into the void.

ASSIGNATION
STELLAR DATE: 02.05.8512 (Adjusted Gregorian)
LOCATION: *Verisimilitude*
REGION: Nesella Station, Regula, Midditerra System

"What a mess," Odis shook his head as he led Katrina through the *Verisimilitude*. "Bloody pirates fought to the end. Even against their own people."

"I think they knew what was coming to traitors," Katrina replied as they stepped over debris strewn across a corridor.

Odis turned to gaze at Katrina, cocking an eyebrow as he did. "Well, technically the Adders who sided with you are the traitors, aren't they?"

Katrina laughed at the MDF colonel, earning a head shake from the man.

Despite his sour attitude, he spoke his mind and didn't hold back. Katrina appreciated that as more and more sycophants seemed to come out of the bulkheads as the days went on.

"Those sorts of things are fluid," Katrina said when her laughter died down. "Especially in a canton like the Adders'. Respect and fealty go to the strong. It's not that much different than the military; the rules for getting to the top are just different."

Odis snorted. "Yeah, I've noticed."

They reached a lift, and Katrina decided that the risk was small enough to allow herself to get into the enclosed space with Odis. When the doors closed, he turned to her, and she had to resist tensing up.

"What are you going to do with Kruger?" Odis asked. "Is he getting the axe, as well?"

"I don't think so." Katrina shook her head. "He was under the control of his AI. Someone either botched the buffers on the implantation, or they did it to him on purpose."

"Fuckin' AIs," Odis swore. "Anyone who lets one of those things inside their head is an idiot."

"I've known a few who weren't," Katrina replied. "There are a lot of good AIs out there."

"Sure, good AIs abound. I have good friends, too. Doesn't mean I want them sharing skull space with me—especially when they can turn me into a meat puppet, and there's nothing I can do about it."

Katrina nodded as the lift doors opened. "I get that."

Odis walked out first, striding down the corridor toward the bridge, but Katrina didn't budge.

There, standing in the passageway, was Admiral Gunter, gun in his mouth. The look of horror that twisted his visage as he looked at her caused Katrina to take a step back.

Then he pulled the trigger, blowing the back of his head off.

But it wasn't his head blowing apart, spraying brains across the bulkhead.

It was Juasa's.

Her eyes were filled with a mixture of pity and remorse as she held the gun in her mouth. As though she were judging Katrina and finding her wanting.

"No…" Katrina whispered, closing her eyes. "That's *not* what happened."

"What was that?" Odis asked, and Katrina opened her eyes once more to see the colonel standing in the corridor where Juasa had been, a look of concern mixed with annoyance on his face.

"Nothing," Katrina replied as she strode out of the lift. "I was just talking with someone else."

"OK, bridge is this way."

Katrina knew the layout of the ship—she'd studied it before the attack—but followed Odis without comment, trying to come to grips with what she'd seen.

It wasn't the first time the image of Juasa's death had flashed before her eyes. It was there every time she tried to sleep. But never like that. Never *accusing* her.

And mixed with Gunter? What in the stars was *that* about? Was it because the man had preferred to die than follow her?

No. He blew the back of his head off so I couldn't keep tapping his implants and learn what else he had planned. The man was just protecting his own interests.

In one light, it was honorable. Or maybe not. He could also have just been taking the coward's way out.

She shook her head to clear the thoughts away, as she and Odis walked onto the bridge to find Norm lounging in the captain's chair.

"Lady Katrina," he said with a grin, rising slowly. "We tried not to ding her up too much. Most of what went down was cosmetic."

"You did good, Norm. Both of you," she nodded to Odis. "A ship like the *'Tude* has no place in Kruger's hands."

"Shouldn't be in the Adders' hands, either," Odis muttered.

"Why's that, soldier-boy?" Norm said, turning to face Odis. "What's wrong with the Adders having our own ship back?"

Odis gave Norm a disdainful look. "Maybe because pirates prowling around other systems with cruisers is bad for business, attracts the wrong kind of attention. But mostly because it was the MDF that took the ship, not you."

Norm took a step toward Odis. "I lost good people securing that dock so you didn't have a hundred guns up your ass."

"I lost good people, too," Odis growled, his voice low and menacing. "But that's what a real military does. We understand that going in."

"Oh? A 'real military'? You get in, what, one or two stand-up fights a century? The Adders are fighting every week. You guys are fucking comedians compared to us."

Katrina folded her arms across her chest as she regarded the two men. "You guys done yet? If you whip your dicks out, I can measure them, if you'd like. I'm not getting 'em hard first, though. That's on you."

Odis shot Katrina a look of revulsion, while Norm's face showed shock for a minute, before he burst out laughing. The MDF colonel didn't join in, but his ire faded a touch.

"I need force cohesion," Katrina said, once Norm got himself under control. "That starts with you two getting along. Neither could have pulled this off without the other. Sam was instrumental, as well. But if I take the

Adders' flagship and turn it over to the MDF, we're going to have a repeat of what we just went through." She looked to Odis as she finished the statement. "Understood?"

Odis nodded, and she could see that he did understand.

"Good. Remember, we could be just days away from an attack by one of our neighbors, or even from Bollam's World."

"Bollam's? Really?" Norm asked.

"It's possible." Odis glanced at the pirate. "Especially if they want our new, illustrious leader badly enough."

"They want my ship," Katrina replied. "We're alike in that respect."

Norm's gaze danced between the two. "If we're so worried about an attack from the Bollers, what's your plan, Lady Katrina?"

"Well, we don't know anything other than that it's a risk. Which means we can't leave any approach unguarded." Katrina looked to Odis. "Colonel, how do you feel about a field promotion?"

"Like I'm about to have a very serious headache. Isn't there someone in Gunter's command that you can put in charge of his fleet?"

"I trust you, Odis."

"Stars, I have no idea why. You didn't put your tech in my head, did you?"

Katrina shook her head. "No. I'm actively trying not to do that anymore."

"I suppose that's a little reassuring. Fine. Make me an admiral. I'll run Gunter's fleet, but you'd better sit down with his command officers and make it clear to them that they're listening to me. I don't want to spend the next few weeks in pissing matches."

"Why not?" Norm asked. "You're so good at them."

"Boys..."

VOYAGER
STELLAR DATE: 02.06.8512 (Adjusted Gregorian)
LOCATION: *Voyager*
REGION: Scattered Disk, Midditerra System

Troy watched the crew in the cockpit of the *Voyager*. They were reviewing the data they'd pulled from the Midditerra System's beacons, and from comm signals that were strong enough to reach out into the void.

"That's…that's a thing," Carl said, after they'd all listened to a message declaring the attempted power-grab by Jace defeated, and proclaiming Katrina ruler of the Midditerra System.

"She doesn't seem to mess around," Camille added. "I mean, we knew that she'd taken charge, but this is something else."

"Brutal," Kirb said quietly. "The word you're looking for is 'brutal'."

Rama looked at Kirb. "I'm not filled with sympathy; you know how this filth operates. Stars, they're probably using most of our friends from the *Havermere* as slaves."

"Hopefully not anymore," Kirb replied. "If Katrina's in charge now, I'd like to think that she's freed them."

<Don't count on it.> Troy inserted himself into the conversation. *<She's going to be mighty low on allies. She'll have to be careful what fights she picks.>*

"Plus, she was betrayed by half the people on the *Havermere*." Carl gave the rest of the humans a level look.

127

"She'd better not have mistreated Mandy," Camille replied. "She wasn't in on it."

<We'll find out soon enough. Let's not get worked up about things that we can't help right now,> Troy cautioned.

"Do we have to wait?" Rama asked. "If Katrina is in charge, we can just fly right in—"

"Not so fast," Carl said, shaking his head. "Like Troy said, she's probably not in a terribly secure situation. If we wander into the system, we stand a good chance of screwing everything up."

"Fine." Rama folded her arms and glared at Carl. "I just want this all to be over."

<Well, you did want to leave the Bollam's World System and have a grand adventure,> Troy said, sending a grin into the crew's minds. <This is what grand adventures are like.>

"I didn't want a 'grand' adventure," Camille said with a soft laugh. "I would have settled for a regular adventure. Heck, even some simple sightseeing would have done the trick."

"So what do we do, then?" Kirb asked.

<We need more intel,> Troy replied. <Ideally to find out where Katrina is, and see if we can tightbeam her a message. I can set up an encrypted channel that only she'll be able to listen to, but I don't want to broadcast our position to the entire system.>

"Whoa!" Camille shouted. "What the hell is this?"

Troy saw that she was reviewing scan, and pulled it up on the main holo.

Passive scan had picked up a host of engine flares less than an AU from the *Voyager*'s current position. Without active sweeps, it was difficult to tell them all apart, but he estimated that there were at least four hundred ships.

"Shit," Carl whispered. "Those are Bollam's World SF drive signatures."

"Wow! They came all the way here?" Camille ran a hand through her hair, glancing worriedly at the other humans. "That's some serious dedication."

<Four hundred ships is hardly enough to take this system,> Troy mused. *<Either this is a scouting party, or it's a diversion.>*

"Four hundred ships may not be a huge force, but it's almost overkill for either of those purposes," Carl replied.

"They haven't spotted us, have they?" Rama asked.

"Doubt it, Rams." Camille leant over to pat the other woman on the shoulder. "None of their ships have turned. With their engine wash headed this way, they don't stand a chance of spotting us. No way, no how."

<All the same, when the ionized plasma reaches us, it's going to overwhelm our rad benders, and our stealth will fail. Let's get on the move before then.>

"Well, at least there's one good thing about our friends from the BWSF showing up," Carl said, a smile on his lips.

"Oh?" Camille asked. "What's that?"

"It'll flush out Katrina."

Troy suspected that he was right, but it could just as easily result in her becoming completely inaccessible—or being killed.

INTO THE FLAMES
STELLAR DATE: 02.06.8512 (Adjusted Gregorian)
LOCATION: *Castigation*
REGION: Nesella Station, Regula, Midditerra System

Katrina opened her eyes and stared at the overhead in her cabin, wishing she could figure out how to sleep with her eyes open.

"I suppose it's possible," she whispered to herself. "Though I doubt that would help my dreams."

Granted, she'd barely slept enough to dream over the last few days, anyway. The visions of Juasa had gotten worse, mixed with Gunter, Lara, Hana, and others she'd killed, or simply maimed.

Even Malorie appeared before Katrina when she attempted to sleep, the woman's organic head atop her insectile, robot body, accusing her of ruining everything.

"Maybe I did," Katrina muttered. "But you ruined it first."

Juasa appeared before her again, her face centimeters from Katrina's own, a smile on her lips. Katrina could almost smell Juasa's breath, her warm musk, feel her hair falling around them both, tickling her ears.

"Oh, Ju," Katrina whispered. "I'm so sorry...I don't even know what I'm doing anymore. What's the point of all this?"

"You could be happy," Juasa whispered. "You could forget all of this, just leave."

"Where?" Katrina asked. "Where could I go that this all wouldn't happen again?"

Juasa's eyes were kind and forgiving as she looked down at Katrina. "Come be with me, Katrina. Forget this world. Forget Midditerra, Troy, Tanis, the *Intrepid*. Leave it all behind and come be with me forever."

Katrina felt tears streaking her cheeks. She knew Juasa wasn't real. She was imagining this, right? Did that mean that she wanted to kill *herself*?

Juasa faded away, and Katrina felt even emptier than before.

"How messed up am I, that seeing my dead lover encouraging me to kill myself is comforting?"

She wiped the tears from her face, and rolled onto her side, giving her back a break from the pain of laying on it. Initially, Katrina had shunted the pain from her 'skin' away when sleeping, but she found that after spending her days with the constant pain, trying to sleep without it created a loud emptiness in her mind.

It didn't make any sense. She wondered if somehow the change she'd wrought on herself had created some of the psychological issues she now clearly dealt with.

"Except I'm fucking stuck like this," she whispered. "Maybe I could get the medtable from Revenence Castle up to the *Castigation* and take a long flight across the system while it puts me back together again."

Katrina paused, realizing that she was talking aloud. She wondered what that said about her.

She'd not found any better medical tech in Nesella, and even the MDF didn't have anything as good as Malorie and Jace's medtable. *Loot from some raid on an advanced ship or system*, she guessed, *superior to what the rest of Midditerra has available.*

"I'm not going to kill myself," she whispered, saying it aloud to drive the point home. "I'm not. I didn't survive the sithri fields to quit now."

<Katrina!> Sam's voice entered her mind, and for a moment she worried he had been listening in her cabin.

<What?> she asked.

<A fleet has jumped in.>

"Shit!" Katrina exclaimed as she leapt out of bed and rushed out of the room. <How long ago?>

<They're only five AU stellar west of here.>

That meant they'd been in the system for at least forty minutes. Long enough to assess the general state of things.

<Vector?> Katrina asked, before she remembered that she could pull scan data directly.

Stars, I'm really out of it.

<They're headed for Teegarten Station,> Sam replied. His tone was kind, far more than usual. She wondered if he *had* been listening to the audio pickups in her cabin.

"Teegarten," Katrina muttered as she brought up the data on the fleet. <Those are Bollam's World ships.>

<That's what it looks like. Seems as though they've come to find us.>

Katrina reached the lift and waited for the doors to open, barely aware of the world around her as she looked over the enemy vessels.

<So small,> she mused.

<It's over four hundred ships. Not huge, but I don't think you can call that 'so small',> Sam replied.

The lift arrived, thankfully empty, and Katrina stepped on, not bothering to tell it where to go. Sam would take it to the bridge. He was perhaps the one person she could trust implicitly in the entire system.

<*Not the number of ships, the classes,*> Katrina said. <*I wouldn't rate the biggest one as more than a light cruiser.*>

<*I noted that, as well. Just a scouting force?*>

<*Scouting forces usually scout and then leave. They don't attack,*> Katrina replied as the lift doors opened.

<*Then, what?*> Sam asked.

"It's a feint. Has to be," Katrina replied aloud as she walked onto the bridge.

Jordan was already there, sitting in the captain's chair and pulling her hair—which looked like it hadn't seen a brush in a day—back into a messy bun.

"Your friends are here," she said to Katrina by way of greeting.

"Noticed that," Katrina replied.

"I have Admiral Odis," Paula said from the comm station.

"Put him on the tank," Katrina replied.

"Lady Katrina, Captain Jordan," Odis said when he appeared. "Looks like the Bollers are trying to draw us out."

"Is that your assessment?" Katrina asked. "A feint to pull us from the more valuable stations?"

Odis gave a curt nod. "It is, Lady Katrina. A force that size is just large enough that it's more than a smaller station like Teegarten can defend against. It requires fleet movement to answer it, but that will weaken other defenses."

"It's annoyingly clever," Katrina replied. "It telegraphs the attack, but is just as likely to make us do something stupid as mount an effective defense. We have, what, sixty ships close to Teegarten?"

"Sixty-seven," Odis replied.

"And the ships that the cantons have sent? There are a dozen headed this way—can we divert them? With the station's defenses, that may be enough to hold the Bollers back."

"Maybe." Odis appeared to be considering options. "Or maybe we just lose all those ships, and they repeat the strategy, hitting another station we can't adequately defend."

Katrina wished she were anywhere but on the bridge of the *Castigation*. Anywhere but in position to be responsible for the lives of millions. Millions of people she didn't really like, people she had no business ruling over.

"Admiral Odis. Contact the Teegarten Stationmaster. Signal a general evacuation. There's nothing we can do for them."

"A million people live on Teegarten," Jordan said quietly.

"I know," Katrina replied. "But there are three hundred million on Nesella. Even more on Uriah. Do we abandon them to protect Teegarten?"

"They won't all be able to get off," Odis said, his voice solemn. "Teegarten isn't exactly known for following safety protocols and keeping enough evac ships onhand."

Katrina scrubbed her palms against her face, leaving them there as she spoke. "I'm open to options. Lay a plan on me."

Odis was silent for a moment, his lips pressed tightly together. He stroked his chin. "Well, with the enemy's current vector, they have a straight shot at Teegarten. But if they are forced to slow enough, it would allow the station to pass behind Kora in its orbit. That would give us enough time to get more ships there to defend—or facilitate evac."

Katrina brought up Teegarten and Kora, the planet it orbited, on a secondary holo, then expanded the view to show the approaching Bollam's World ships.

"They'll have already fired an initial kinetic salvo."

Odis nodded. "They have. We picked it up. We've not managed to track every shot, but we've detected about half. The ships in that sector are moving in to take out incoming rounds as best they can.

Katrina pulled up the MDF ships that were in range of Teegarten.

"Sixty-seven ships against over four hundred...what about the canton-owned ships docked at Teegarten? There are eighty of them."

"Some are already leaving," Jordan said. "A lot are legitimate freighters."

"They better not leave until they take evacuees," Katrina growled. "Jordan pass an order to the stationmaster to deny debarkation to ships that don't take passengers. Tell them to come to Nesella."

"I'll pass the order, but the stationmaster will have a hell of a time enforcing it."

Katrina knew that to be true, but if they could save a few extra people, it would be worthwhile.

"Teegarten's going to be total chaos," Odis commented.

"Yeah," Katrina shot back, "War has a way of doing that. This isn't like exercises or sims. It's the real world, and we're in the shit. We have to suck it up and deal with it."

Odis's expression grew stony, but he nodded in acknowledgement.

"OK," Katrina gestured to the holo. "Of those sixty-seven ships, we have three cruisers. Those suckers can pack a punch. If we form the ships into three groups, we can harry the Bollers and slow their approach."

"It's risky," Odis replied. "Rails are our only good option at that range. I don't know how much we can slow them down."

"Like I said," Katrina fixed the admiral with a level stare. "I'm open to options. The station can fire on them, too."

Odis regarded her silently for half a minute, and Katrina turned away, looking to the holodisplay and wishing she had some inkling as to where the main attack would hit. That would tell her from where she could pull resources.

Granted, that would just change the target of the main attack.

Stars…what I wouldn't give to have Troy's computational power. He'd be able to map out the whole thing, give me probabilities on every option. This feels like we're planning a battle with pen and paper.

<I've been conferring with the MDF tactical AIs and NSAIs,> Sam said to the group. <We have come up with

136

firing patterns from the MDF ships that can work, but we need two more cruisers to pull it off.>

Odis's mouth set in a firm line, and Katrina knew he wouldn't agree to reconfigure his force—not without a fight.

"We'll do it," Katrina replied. The *Castigation* and the *Verisimilitude*. Sam, run the numbers with those ships added."

<On it.>

"That's a huge risk for you," Odis said, his voice not belying whether or not he thought it would please him to see her in harm's way.

"You're telling me," Jordan said with a soft grunt. "But we're up for it. Kicking ass is what we do here."

Katrina caught the dig at the MDF, and she gave Jordan a stern look and sent privately, *<Those sixty-seven ships forming up around Teegarten are putting it all on the line, too.>*

Jordan's response was noncommittal. *<Yeah, I guess.>*

<It can work,> Sam said to the group. *<You'll need to move now. I've passed vector to the* Verisimilitude's *helm. Say the word, Katrina.>*

Katrina glanced at Odis. "Don't say I never did anything for this system."

A small smile graced Odis's lips. "Show me what that looks like, Warlord."

<Norm, you got a vector from Sam. Get the 'Tude on that burn. I'll brief you in a few minutes.>

Norm's response was instantaneous. *<I think I can see what it's all about. We'll be ready to roll in five.>*

137

THE TEMPTRESS
STELLAR DATE: 02.06.8512 (Adjusted Gregorian)
LOCATION: Katrina's Command Room
REGION: Farsa Station, Persia, Midditerra System

Korin drummed his fingers on the arm of Katrina's chair—throne, if he was honest with himself—as he waited for Lady Armis to arrive.

He glanced down at the cylinder to his right and held back a shudder of revulsion. After he'd realized what was in the case Katrina had carried to the council meeting, he could imagine what was in the other cylinder resting beside him.

Jace's brain. Probably.

Korin had never liked Jace much. The man was a boor who tried to behave like a human being from time to time. He'd liked Malorie more. Though she could be cold-hearted, he knew there was a real person deep down inside.

Somehow—despite the fact that there was a human brain floating in a nutrient bath next to him—Jace's presence wasn't as disturbing as the two a-grav columns that held Lara and Hana.

Both of the women were suspended in mid-air, life-support tubing running out of ports in their abdomens. Their eyes were closed—he assumed they were unable to open them—and they never opened their mouths, but their chests rose and fell in a slow rhythm.

At present, the pair were breathing in unison, though he'd noticed it wasn't always the case.

139

"Stars, I wish I could throw a sheet over them," he muttered to himself. "Or at least put them out of their misery."

To his surprise, he saw Lara's hand twitch, and he realized that the woman might be able to hear him. He was about to rise and approach her, when Astrid, Farsa Station's administrative AI, informed him that Lady Armis had arrived.

<Send her in.> Korin sat back and lifted his right leg to lay his ankle across his left knee.

There, this should look imposing enough.

A moment later, Armis strode into the room—alone, as he'd ordered. Even without any guards or attendants, the woman moved as though she commanded everything around her.

Her hair was an iridescent blue, and cascaded over her shoulders like a shimmering waterfall. She wore a long green dress, just the right hue to augment her hair, the look almost making her appear as though she were a forest glade, drifting into the stark room and lighting it up with her presence.

"Commander Korin," Lady Armis said, inclining her head in respect. "Thank you for agreeing to see me."

"Lady Armis." Korin did not rise as she approached. "I assume you're here to turn Lady Marion over to me?"

"Commander. You don't really think I took a grave personal risk in rescuing her only to turn her over, do you?"

Korin shrugged. "Was worth a shot."

Armis laughed. "I suppose it was. Gets it out of the way, too. Marion has claimed sanctuary with me. Until

140

there is a proper tribunal, there she will stay. And with Katrina away, we'll just have to wait."

"If not to discuss Lady Marion, what is the purpose of your visit?" Korin asked. "I don't have authority from Katrina to handle matters of state."

"No, I suppose not," Armis said, glancing at Lara and Hana. "I have to say. I really am not a fan of Katrina's taste in decorations."

Korin couldn't help a small grimace, and Armis spotted it.

"Neither are you, I see."

"I say kill them or free them."

"Oh?" Armis arched an eyebrow. "Life imprisonment isn't an option?"

"Often, a sentence like that is only marginally less cruel than what they're experiencing now. Unless they escape. Then you may as well have freed them to begin with. Best to just end it."

"How pragmatic of you," Armis replied, looking the two women up and down once more. "Tell me, can they hear us?"

"I suspect they can, yes," Korin replied. "Though I wonder how sane they are anymore."

<No matter,> Armis said privately to Korin. <Let us finish our conversation directly. I'd rather they not hear it — though it involves them.>

<What are you playing at, Armis?> Korin asked, tired of the canton ruler's equivocation.

<I know you're loyal to Katrina,> Armis began. <But I have doubts over her suitability to rule Midditerra. In the past few weeks, we've seen far more brutality from her than from

any other system leader in a long time. Despite her graft, Lara was a far better governess.>

<She extorted everyone all the time,> Korin replied. <At least with Katrina, you know what you're getting.>

<Yes, mind control and orbital strikes on the innocent.>

Korin clenched his teeth at the thought of what Katrina had done at Selkirk. He understood the point she had been trying to make, but chances were that the people in that factory were completely innocent.

His own family had been pawns of the canton rulers as far back as any of them knew. Seeing Katrina casually murder unsuspecting citizens had caused him to realize that she was not a significant improvement.

Not to mention the list of names he perseverated over constantly—the Adders he'd lost, taking Kurgise for reasons he still didn't fully understand.

Still, Korin knew he was no saint. He'd committed more than a few cruel acts during his time as a guard at Revenence Castle.

We do what we have to.

When he didn't reply to her charges, Armis took a step closer and leant in, her eyes boring into his. <*Does she have you under her mind control?*>

Korin shook his head. <*No, she never needed to. She doesn't do that to everyone. Careful, though. I'm really starting to get the impression you aren't a fan of Lady Katrina.*>

Armis nodded and straightened. <*Was Lara great? No. But she was a known quantity. Jace was an ass, but Malorie kept things running well enough.*>

Korin snorted. *<Your version of 'well enough' is different than mine. I recall getting orders to beat slaves on a regular basis.>*

*<You were one of Malorie's personal guards. How often did it really happen that **you** were sent out for such tasks?>*

<More often than you'd think.>

Armis didn't reply, but she shifted her stance from one that was subtly alluring to one that was more commanding. Not that she wasn't still alluring.

Not that Korin was foolish enough to think that anyone in the Midditerra System wasn't out for number one. Armis wanted something from him, that much was obvious.

<Well, I don't know if you are aware of how things are done in Canton Draus, but we're not like the others. There are no slaves in Draus.>

Korin found that hard to believe. *<I've seen the reports. You have slaves, in droves.>*

<We lie so that people don't flee the other cantons. It's how the council has allowed Canton Draus to make changes without punishment. Yes, there are some indentured workers, but they're all on a path to earning freedom—a necessary step in the process.>

<Well, shit...> Korin wondered if it was true. *Could Armis really have made a free canton, right under everyone's noses?*

<Look at Lara and Hana, here.> Armis gestured at the two women hanging in a-grav columns. *<Sure, Katrina did what she had to do. I get that, I really do. But she's not making anything better. She's just making the bad shit into **different** bad shit.>*

143

Korin knew she had a point, but he didn't want to admit it. Not yet. Not without proof, at least.

<Look at what she's been doing in the outer system,> Armis continued. *<She killed an admiral, attacked a ship, and now we have the Bollers sending fleets at us. You know what they want. Her.>*

The thought had crossed Korin's mind. If the Bollers got Katrina, they would probably leave. They had no reason to engage in a protracted battle with the MDF and the cantons. But it seemed that they *were* willing to commit resources to get Katrina.

<Am I just to take your word for all this?> Korin asked.

<I'd love to take you down to Draus for the grand tour, but with the Bollers attacking, we need to move fast. I've formed an alliance with Lord Derrick and Lady Jeshis. Derrick is going to hold the homefront, while Jeshis and I take our cantons' fleets out to confront Katrina and turn her over to the Bollers.>

Korin felt his mouth go slack. *There it is.* Armis had laid it out for him; she was talking treason.

Which didn't seem to bother Korin as much as it should.

He laughed softly. *Maybe I'm forming a habit.*

<If we do this, what happens then?> Korin asked.

*<It won't be an overnight change, but I'll work to free all the peoples of Midditerra. This can't remain a pirate's cove. The surrounding systems are steadily recovering from the last wars; if we don't start behaving like civilized people, they **will** band together and crush us.>*

<But you'll free the slaves?> Korin asked. He had to hear Armis say it.

<Yes. I'll free the slaves. Once Katrina is dealt with, and I have control of the council and the MDF.>

Out of the corner of his eyes, he saw Hana twitch, her brows pinching together.

<If I were to go along with this, how do we deal with the AIs? They all support Katrina.>

Armis shrugged. *<AIs aren't people. And if you turn off their power, they aren't anything at all.>*

A SURPRISING PLAN
STELLAR DATE: 02.07.8512 (Adjusted Gregorian)
LOCATION: *Castigation*
REGION: Approaching Kora, Midditerra System

The *Castigation* and *Verisimilitude* drew within two light seconds of the MDF ships protecting Teegarten, finally close enough for real-time communication—albeit with an annoying lag.

Katrina pulled up the MDF Flight Commanders on the *Castigation*'s holodisplay.

All three were colonels who had previously served under Admiral Gunter, and now Odis. She suspected that one of them, Colonel Myla, felt as though she should have taken Gunter's place.

The woman may have been right. Odis's reticence hadn't diminished with his promotion. If anything, it had increased. Colonel Myla, on the other hand, had fire in her belly and was more than ready to beat the Bollers back.

"Lady Katrina. I like what the AIs have come up with," Myla said as soon as the holodisplay came online. "But it's too passive. We can hit the Bollers hard. Push them back."

Katrina shook her head. Maybe there was *too* much fire in Myla's belly. "Remember, Colonel Myla, this is not the only attack we're bound to face. They've already launched kinetic salvos at over a dozen stations. Some are even headed toward Persia and Farsa."

Myla gave a dismissive wave of her hand. "Those are of no concern; the canton ships around Persia can take them out. But if we let these Bollers destroy Teegarten, they're going to be emboldened. They'll hit harder. Stopping them here is paramount."

"I don't disagree," Katrina replied. "But what do you have to offer that doesn't weaken us elsewhere?"

"Not a lot," Colonel Safra said with a snort. "If willpower was enough, Myla would push them back herself, but we just don't have the ships for this."

"They only have five light cruisers in the formation," Colonel Greg added. "We have eight light cruisers, and now five cruisers. We outclass them, and we have Teegarten's rails."

Katrina had considered more aggressive options on the flight from Nesella to Teegarten. She would like nothing more than to kick the Bollam's World fleet back into the dark layer, but she couldn't work out a way to do it that didn't sacrifice the majority of her ships.

And if she failed, there would be no one to shepherd the fleeing civilians.

For a moment, Katrina saw Juasa's face hovering before her.

"I *knew* you cared," the visage said before smiling kindly.

Katrina blinked it away as Myla replied to Greg.

"We have the canton ships. At least thirty have weapons on par with a destroyer. They—"

"Wait," Katrina said. "What are *those*, on Teegarten?"

"What are what?" Jordan asked.

Katrina pulled up a visual of the station, as it was retreating around the back of the planet on its orbit.

"Those two ships. Docked at the bottom of the station's central spire."

"Sexy, aren't they?" Jordan grinned. "Those are a pair of planet pushers that Canton Selkirk stole almost a hundred years ago. I forget who from, but they got in a tax dispute with the MDF leader at the time, and the ships ended up there. They've been an off and on point of contention, but neither side wanted to give, so they just sit in Teegarten's impound."

"Do they work?" Katrina asked.

"They've been scavenged. A lot," Colonel Safra said. "I'd be shocked if the lights turned on."

<Demy,> Katrina called down to engineering. *<What do you know about those two heavy tugs at the bottom of Teegarten.>*

<They're a damn shame, is what they are. Those are FGT pushers! No one's ever figured out where Selkirk got them from, but they're some of the most beautiful things these two eyes have ever gazed upon.>

Katrina couldn't help a small laugh. *<You get really eloquent when talking about starships, Demy.>*

<Yeah, what can I say? Want to get me riled up, show me a smooth-running AP drive.>

Katrina only paid half a mind to the three colonels as they argued over small alterations to Sam's plan. *<Do you think they still work?>*

<Stars, Lady Katrina, I don't know. I mean…they flew in under their own steam a century ago, but I doubt they would now.>

<We don't need them to fly across the system. We just need to push Teegarten into a higher—and slower—orbit.>

Demy didn't reply for almost a minute, and Katrina knew the woman was reviewing options. While she waited, she returned her focus to the colonels.

"Right," Greg was saying to Myla. "I'll just sacrifice all my ships so you can get the glory. That sounds great."

"Well, someone has to do something!" Myla yelled back. "We've gotta protect the station. We all know that they'll only be able to evac a fraction of the people."

"I might have something that can buy us time," Katrina interjected.

"Oh yeah?" Myla asked, and Katrina raised an eyebrow. Myla lowered her voice, adding a modicum more respect. "Lady Katrina."

"We might be able to move the station to a higher orbit, much more quickly than the enemy would expect."

"Are you referring to those planet pushers?" Colonel Safra asked. "Like I said, they've been scavenged heavily."

"My engineer is a miracle worker," Katrina replied, keeping her voice calm and even. *<Demy, do you have anything?>*

*<I **think** I might. But I need to get over there with a team immediately.>*

<Do it.>

"Colonels," Katrina let a smile creep across her lips. "Let's put together a plan that assumes Teegarten never comes back around the planet."

DEFENSE OF TEEGARTEN
STELLAR DATE: 02.07.8512 (Adjusted Gregorian)
LOCATION: *Castigation*
REGION: Kora, Midditerra System

Katrina stood next to the weapons console on the *Castigation*'s bridge, watching the holo tanks as the first kinetic rounds streaked past the Boller ships.

The MDF fleet was spread out four light seconds from the planet, grouped to protect the three cruisers. The *Castigation* and the *Verisimilitude* were in position above and below the planet, waiting for their turn to join in the fight.

The enemy had detected the incoming rail-shots, and shifted to avoid the strikes, but as the MDF ships and Teegarten Station continued to fire on them, the enemy had to spread out further, relying on jinking patterns to make their vectors unpredictable.

"It's working," Jordan said from the captain's chair. "They're shedding more and more *v*."

The enemy ships were now five light seconds from the Boller vessels. The three MDF flights were moving perpendicular to the enemy fleet, the Midditerran ships moving away from the path of the incoming vessels.

The MDF colonels hadn't fully grasped Katrina's plan at first, but once they saw the advantage it gave, they'd been enthusiastic about the improved chances of success.

Of course, it would all be for naught if Demy couldn't get the FGT planet pushers to light up. The plan also assumed that the Bollers would take the most expeditious route around the planet.

So many 'ifs', Katrina thought as she watched the three MDF flights report readiness to fire. This was the most risky part of the defense. If the Bollers decided that wiping out the MDF defenders was a priority over taking out Teegarten, it would change everything.

Even though most of the four hundred ships in the Boller fleet were destroyers, they could still crush the sixty ships the MDF was bracketing them with.

But in order to move on vectors to engage the MDF flights, the Bollers would have to brake hard, exposing their unshielded engines to the defensive rail guns around Kora.

Truth be told, the enemy wouldn't lose many ships, but their losses would be greater than if they'd arced around the planet, destroyed Teegarten, and then looped back to deal with the MDF fleet afterward.

"Take the easy route," Katrina whispered.

"Are you worried they won't?" Jordan asked.

Katrina shrugged. "I'll worry about it 'til the deed is done. I still wonder where the rest of their fleet is."

"What if it's not anywhere?" Jordan asked. "What if they're just faking us out?"

"Well, our plan is to win this. So if that's the case, we just win it and save the day, versus winning it and having that only be the start of our troubles."

"So you're going for a win-win?" Jordan said with a laugh.

"They're engaging," the Adder on scan announced. "Bollers are firing beams at max range, our ships are jinking. Not firing back yet."

"Good," Katrina replied, glad to see that the MDF colonels were following the plan.

The enemy was firing beams right at the hundred-thousand-kilometer range. Scan showed their weapons being deflected by the MDF's shields, though not as well as she'd like. The MDF ships weren't jinking widely enough, and some were taking repeated hits from Boller weapons.

Karina saw that it was Myla's flight that was not jinking enough and taking the most hits.

"Myla…" Katrina whispered. "What are you doing?"

"She's braking," Scan announced. "Moving closer to the Boller ships."

"She's going to try to engage directly! What the fuck?" Jordan swore.

<Myla! What are you doing?> Katrina sent the message, knowing she'd have to wait over ten seconds for the response.

Katrina watched as the twenty ships in Myla's flight eased toward the Boller fleet, weathering in increasing barrage of beams.

<I'm going to take out enough of these bastards to make them think twice about attacking Midditerra,> Myla responded after the delay.

"What does she think—" Jordan asked, then stopped as it became apparent what Myla was up to.

"That lying bitch." Katrina clenched her teeth 'til her jaw ached. "Myla had RMs all along—I flat-out asked if we had any available."

"Glory hound," Jordan scoffed.

<Three of Myla's ships have suffered shield breaches,> Sam announced. *<Five now.>*

On the holo, one of Myla's ships suddenly winked out, and Katrina pulled up an optical view. It showed the ship's shields flare, then a beam tearing through the MDF destroyer, flames and atmosphere pouring out of the holes in its hull. A moment later, something exploded within the ship, turning it into a cloud of shrapnel.

"Fuck," Katrina whispered.

"Tracking twenty RMs," Scan announced.

"That's a fortune in missiles," Jordan said, scowling at the holotank.

Katrina could feel rage overtaking her. "That fool. Firing RMs at close-range from known sources on known targets…"

<Less than half will make it to their destinations,> Sam reported.

Sure enough, scan showed ten of the RMs wink out before they even reached the midway point. Moments later, two more were destroyed.

"Relativistic missiles are a fucking waste if they don't have time to hit relativistic speeds," Katrina muttered as the remaining eight missiles reached their targets and detonated successfully.

Myla had targeted the enemy's light cruisers, and three missiles hit one, the explosions clouding the ship.

When scan could get a clear reading, they saw the vessel's shields had failed—though it was otherwise undamaged.

The remaining five missiles struck another cruiser, the initial two disabling its shields, and the final three obliterating the ship.

A small consolation for such a large expenditure of ordnance.

A moment later, beams from the MDF ships lanced through the void, striking the ship without shields, holing it thoroughly. Katrina nodded with satisfaction as it began to spin from the flames and atmosphere shooting into space.

During the exchange, the BWSF ships had not sat idle. Another five of Myla's destroyers were now drifting hulks, and two of Greg's had joined them.

<Pull away,> Katrina ordered the three colonels. <Let them pass and re-engage from the rear.>

Acknowledgements came back a few seconds later, and Katrina was glad Myla hadn't sent back a verbal message. It would have prompted her to give the woman a brutal tongue lashing.

Despite the losses, the engagement had created the desired result. The enemy ships were close to Kora's equatorial plane. They'd pass around the planet, expecting to see Teegarten in one place, only to find it in another.

Hopefully.

Katrina sent a signal via relay to the *Verisimilitude*, which lay within the planet's clouds, hovering over its southern pole. Four MDF ships and a dozen canton frigates were in position with it, a similar grouping to those in position with the *Castigation* in the clouds over the north pole.

<Get ready, Norm,> she warned. *<We have to be sure to drive them around the eastern side of Kora.>*

<Aye, Warlord,> came Norm's steady response.

Katrina hoped he would follow the plan. Myla had already wasted over ten percent of the MDF fleet to take out less than one percent of the enemy's.

If Demy couldn't light those planet pusher's engines, even the fallback plan would be at serious risk.

The BWSF ships closed within two light-seconds of the planet, and Katrina saw their formation split to come around both sides.

<Flight Four, break cover, hit those ships on the left flank!>

Jordan called out orders, and the *Castigation* surged out of Kora's clouds, beams and rails firing into the enemy formation. Jordan was following orders to the letter, targeting the destroyers, trying to create as much confusion as possible. The other ships in their flight followed suit, coordinating their fire with the *Castigation*'s, destroying three enemy ships in the initial salvo.

Jordan was engaging new targets as the *Verisimilitude* and Flight Five joined the fray. The concentrated fire, aimed at the BWSF destroyers and *not* their light cruisers, took out ship after ship on the left flank, driving the enemy back over the western side of the planet.

Flights four and five boosted toward one another, crossing over Kora's equator, still harrying the enemy ships, which were firing back—some shots between ships at ranges as close as five thousand kilometers.

"Fucking fuck!" Jordan cursed as a kinetic salvo hammered the *Castigation*, overwhelming one of the shield umbrellas. "Rotate us," she called out to helm.

"On it," Helm replied as the ship spun on its axis, putting the damaged shields on the far side of the ship as more weapons fire struck the *Castigation*. Most of it was coming from a pair of enemy light cruisers that were advancing on Flight Four while the destroyers peeled away.

<I have to divert power from beams to hold the shields,> Sam announced. <They're pummeling us.>

Katrina was about to order Jordan to pull the *Castigation* back into the planet's clouds when a salvo of missiles struck one of the BWSF cruisers, taking out its dorsal shields. She saw the *Verisimilitude* on approach, the cruiser firing all twenty of its forward beams, cutting the enemy cruiser nearly in half before turning its guns on the other attacker. The remaining BWSF light cruiser altered course and fell back behind the protective shield of the destroyers.

Katrina glanced at Jordan, and both women breathed a sigh of relief. They'd done it. The enemy was passing around the western side of Kora.

Now it was all down to Demy.

BURN AND FEINT
STELLAR DATE: 02.07.8512 (Adjusted Gregorian)
LOCATION: *Castigation*
REGION: Kora, Midditerra System

While the BWSF fleet sped around the western side of Kora, the *Castigation* and Flight Four passed over the planet's southern pole to see Teegarten Station angled with the lower end of its spire pointed at the Bollam's World ships.

At the bottom of the spire, the two FGT planet pushers—a name Katrina knew to be more hyperbole than fact—were in position to push the station away, with their engines aimed at the approaching Boller fleet.

But the great cones were dark; neither the AP drives, nor the fusion burners were emitting any signs of life.

Katrina didn't hold any hopes for the AP engines— getting enough antimatter onto the ships in short order would be a risky proposition in and of itself.

But she'd hoped the fusion drives would work.

<Demy,> Katrina called out. *<Tell me you're about to light them.>*

<Stars, Katrina, just give me one more fucking minute.>

Katrina was shocked at the vehemence in the diminutive woman's voice, but she supposed that answer was better than 'no fucking way'.

<OK. We'll try to stall them.>

The *Verisimilitude* and Flight Five were passing over the north pole, and Katrina signaled them to keep firing on the BWSF fleet. They had to keep the enemy focused on ships and not the station.

As the two flights kept firing on the Bollers, the enemy responded, launching waves of missiles and kinetics at the MDF and canton starships.

"Stars, we can't take much more," Jordan said as the *Castigation* registered another shield failure.

<Demy, now or never, what do you have for us?>

<We've got the lasers online, and the fuel is flowing, just give me one…more…there! Now for the AP!>

Katrina had seen planet pushers burn before, as the *Intrepid* had used them in the Kapteyn's Star System on several occasions. Even so, it was always a sight to behold.

"Mother fucking fuck," Jordan whispered, as their view of Teegarten Station was completely obscured by what could only be described as star-eclipsing light.

The torches coming off the planet pushers were so bright that over fifteen degrees of scan was blinded by them. The engines continued to increase their burn, pouring plasma into space, the wash directed squarely at the approaching BWSF fleet.

It was a churn and burn unlike any Katrina had ever seen.

The enemy ships began to veer off course, pulling up and away from the jets of raw energy pouring off the pushers.

But many of them were not fast enough.

A dozen enemy ships were vaporized before they could even alter vector, and a hundred more lost shields before they could pull away.

"Sam, give the station's guns targeting data, there's no way they'll be able to see through that plume."

<You got it.>

The station's railguns began to fire, joining the Midditerra ships as they pummeled every BWSF vessel whose shields had failed.

As the MDF and canton ships opened fire, there were still over a hundred enemy ships in the plasma wash. Then Demy pulled off the impossible, and ignited the antimatter pion drives, spraying gamma rays out of the pushers, exciting the plasma further and slamming it into the remaining Boller ships.

"Now *that's* how you wipe out an enemy fleet," Katrina said with a wide grin, as the surviving BWSF ships began to break apart into smaller formations, boosting stellar north and south.

There were still over one hundred fifty with working engines and navigation, but many of those had weakened shields. They would be ripe targets for flights one through three, which were beginning to come around Kora's eastern side, bringing heavy fire to bear on the remains of the BWSF fleet.

Katrina watched the Bollam's World ships, wondering if they would dare come back around for another attack. They'd suffered terrible losses, but so had the MDF, and the trick with the pushers would not work a second time.

With the canton vessels, Katrina's force had numbered a hundred, but there were now fewer than fifty Midditerra ships operating under their own power.

As Katrina was evaluating options, the planet pushers shut down their engines, and scan could once again observe Teegarten Station as it moved away from Kora.

The heavy thrust had caused visible damage to two of the rings, and a trail of debris from torn cargo nets and other scaffolding lay in the station's wake. Teegarten was saved, but it might still end up as scrap.

"Did we win?" Jordan asked with a rueful laugh.

"I have—" Katrina began, but Sam interrupted her.

<I've got a strange signal coming in.> Sam sounded perplexed. <It's on one of the Adders' comm frequencies, but none of our decryption algorithms work.>

"Pass it to me," Katrina instructed.

Sam complied, and the moment he did, she identified the origins from the message header.

"Troy…" She could have wept with joy, knowing that he was out there, close enough to send her a signal. A part of her had written him and the *Voyager* off, assuming some terrible fate had befallen them and she'd never see either again. But he was alive.

If Troy was alive, then the ship was likely with him.

"Troy?" Jordan asked, and Katrina realized that she'd said the name aloud.

"A friend," she replied while decrypting the message.

<Katrina, I hope you're OK…you seem to have gone a bit savage, but perhaps that's needed in this crazy system. None of that matters right now. You're fighting a feint. We picked up a beacon that fleet you've engaged left behind. Their main force is going to jump in two hours from when I'm sending this. They'll be at the coordinates I've included, and the smaller fleet has directed them to hit Nesella—since that's where they think

you are. There was a reference to the BWSF Fleet number of the main attack force. Carl and Rama recognized it, and have rough size and composition data. We're staying close, but dark. It seems too dangerous to come insystem right now. Let me know what you want us to do.>

Katrina sucked in a deep breath as she pulled up the data on the main BWSF attack force.

"Shit," she whispered, feeling weak in the knees.

"What is it?" Jordan asked.

Katrina passed the data to Sam and he put it up on the main holo.

<Katrina...this is over four thousand ships. Maybe five, if the supplemental fleet elements come.>

Sam's voice was filled with uncharacteristic levels of worry.

"I know," Katrina replied, turning to Jordan, whose face was ashen. "Captain Jordan. We have to deal with the remains of this fleet quickly so we can get to Nesella. Sam, I need you to broadcast this intel to all insystem vessels. We *must* stop the Bollers at Nesella."

"What if this is just one of the fleets they're sending?" Jordan asked.

"No," Katrina replied. "This is it. It's over a quarter of their home fleet. They wouldn't send more—it would make them too vulnerable. Besides, if they do, we're screwed. That's run-away time."

*<Isn't **now** run-away time?>* Sam asked.

Katrina shook her head, eyes fixed on a vision of Juasa standing next to the main holotank, her eyes filled with accusation.

161

"No." Katrina drew herself up. "Jordan. Recall Demy and her team. Form up with Norm's fifth flight. Take us to these coordinates. I'll direct the colonels and their three flights to escort Teegarten and keep the Bollers off them."

"Why there?" Jordan asked, frowning at the coordinates that Katrina had placed on the holo.

"Just do it, Jordan. OK?"

Jordan shot Katrina a hurt look. "Yeah, on it."

Katrina felt a stab of momentary regret for snapping at Jordan, but she knew the captain wouldn't like the orders that were coming next.

Best to wait 'til the ships are in position before giving it.

CAVALRY
STELLAR DATE: 02.07.8512 (Adjusted Gregorian)
LOCATION: *Castigation*
REGION: Kora, Midditerra System

Seventeen ships formed up at the coordinates Katrina had provided.

However, as Katrina had feared, the surviving Bollam's World ships continued to harass Teegarten Station, though the enemy no longer had enough firepower to close with it—not so long as the surviving MDF ships from flights one through three protected it.

By some perverse miracle, Myla had survived, but Greg and Safra had not.

Katrina put all the remaining ships, twenty-nine in total, under Myla's command and told her to keep Teegarten safe.

"What the hell, Katrina! I can help at Nesella," Myla yelled over the comms after receiving her orders.

"You can *maybe* help there, or you can absolutely keep these people safe here," Katrina replied. "Even if the Bollers bugger off, you still need to organize search and rescue. Half your people are drifting dark in the void. Take some responsibility, Colonel."

Katrina's last statement shut Myla up, barring a final, "Yes, Warlord," before she cut the comm signal.

"OK, Katrina," Jordan said once Katrina's conversation with Myla was over. "We're here. Now what?"

"Now we jump."

"We fucking *what*?" Jordan almost shouted, and every eye on the bridge turned to stare at Katrina.

"Not the whole way," Katrina replied. "Just three AU. There's a route that's clear."

<*Not on any map I have,*> Sam replied.

"It's not something that the canton leaders shared with everyone, but there's a lot they kept off the public maps," Katrina replied as she passed out the updated navigation data.

<*The last time this particular route was verified by drone was four years ago,*> Sam said.

"We're going," Katrina said, her tone brooking no argument. <*Fourth and Fifth flights, we are now designated Cavalry One. We're on course for a three AU jump. Updated nav data has been disseminated. Prepare for jump on my mark.*>

Thirteen ships signaled acknowledgement. Two canton frigates did not—both Selkirk ships—and Katrina sent a message to them.

<*Castigation and the* Verisimilitude *will be jumping last. You jump, or we blow you away. You may not give a shit about this system, but hopefully you do about your lives.*>

There was no verbal response, but both ships signaled acknowledgement. Katrina had no way to believe they wouldn't drop out of the dark layer a minute after transitioning, but it was the most she could do.

<*All ships. Jump.*>

The Fifteen ships disappeared, and then Katrina sent the signal to Norm aboard the *Verisimilitude*. <*OK, Norm, let's go save the day.*>

<*You got it, Lady Katrina.*>

The *Verisimilitude* winked out of normal space. Katrina nodded to Jordan, who swallowed before signaling the *Castigation*'s helm to do likewise.

* * * * *

"I've got multiple contacts, a hundred destroyers, thirty cruisers! They're almost right on top of us!" Scan cried out a moment after the *Castigation* re-entered normal space.

Sam put the data on the main holotank, and Katrina sucked in a deep breath. The main Boller fleet was spread out across five light seconds as they closed on Regula and Nesella station. The enemy was covering all the approaches, and Katrina's small group of ships had jumped right into the middle of them.

Going back into the dark layer wasn't an option; there was no clear path on their current vector

<All ships, pull in tight,> Katrina ordered. <We're going to interlock our shield umbrellas.>

"Shit, Katrina, you just get crazier and crazier," Jordan muttered as she directed helm to follow the order.

Sam helped the vessels coordinate the maneuver. The *Castigation* was at the front of the grouping, and the *Verisimilitude* was at the rear. The middle consisted of five MDF ships and eight canton frigates. Predictably, the two Selkirk vessels were nowhere to be seen.

Cowards. Katrina resolved to hunt them down later — if any of them survived.

<I've only ever heard **rumor** of this being done, you know,> Sam said as the ships shifted into position. <I've also heard that very bad things can happen if it goes wrong.>

She reviewed the positions that Sam had worked out, worried about the stories of shield-interlocks gone wrong. If the overlapping umbrellas were in the wrong positions, she knew they could create a graviton feedback that would crush the ships inside into a singularity.

"We've no choice, Sam." Katrina worked to keep her voice steady. "Either that, or the BWSF squashes us."

The ships of Cavalry One were already taking fire from nearby BWSF destroyers, though not enough to breach shields, and a dozen enemy cruisers were moving into range. They would crush Katrina's ragtag group without any trouble at all.

A few of the ships in her group had been slow to assume the close-in formation. Katrina was about to reach out to their captains, but with the Boller vessels closing, they all dropped into place without further delay.

"At least we got in the fight," Paula muttered derisively from the comm station.

"Shit! Where did that come from?" Scan called out. "There's a ship...a weird ship...coming right at us."

Katrina turned to the holotank and could have wept tears of joy as she saw the *Voyager*'s profile show up on scan.

"They're signaling us," Paula called out. "Should I—"

"Yes!" Katrina shouted.

<Katrina!> Troy's voice came into her mind. *<What are you doing, you're going to get crushed!>*

<It's an interlocked shield maneuver, it'll be en—>

<Not like that, it won't,> Troy shot back. *<You'll all die if you try. OK, who's the AI running things over there?>*

<That'd be me,> Sam replied, his mental tone sounding both relieved and mildly defensive. *<Well, I wouldn't say I'm **running** things.>*

<Sam! Glad you're still around!> Troy replied, sounding genuinely pleased. *<OK, let me manage positions.>*

Katrina watched with barely contained glee as the *Voyager* boosted toward her group. From what the nav NSAI plotted out, her long-lost ship would reach Cavalry One's formation five seconds before the BWSF vessels had firing solutions.

<I'm feeding Sam new positions,> Troy announced a moment later. *<And we're slaving all the ships' shield control systems to him. Stars, this shit is primitive.... I don't even know how these asshats manage to fly in the black.>*

<Troy, you have no idea how good it is to hear you complain about things,> Katrina laughed

<It's good to hear your voice, too. Now let me focus.>

"So that's your ship?" Jordan asked looking over the approaching vessel on scan. "It's all scuffed up and ratty looking."

"Looks like it's been through the wringer," Katrina replied, wondering what had befallen the *Voyager*. "I sure hope they did it to disguise the ship. If Troy damaged her…"

"I think it's cosmetic," Jordan said, rising from her chair and approaching the holotank. "I don't see any actual damage anywhere."

<Katrina,> a new voice reached out to her, and she recognized Carl, Juasa's right-hand man on the *Havermere.* <Stars, we're glad to finally reach you. Well, maybe 'glad' is the wrong word, considering what we're in the middle of. Is Juasa OK?>

A painful lump formed in Katrina's throat, and she was glad that an audible response wasn't needed. She doubted it would be possible.

<She...> Katrina managed to get out, before Juasa appeared before her. She was smiling, but looked sad. Words failed Katrina, and she leant against a console.

After a moment, Carl replied. <I'm so sorry, Katrina. What about the rest of the *Havermere's* crew? And Mandy?>

<A lot of them were involved in Anna's betrayal. Most of them are gone. A few are on my ship here. Mandy was killed by Anna, though.>

Carl made a strange choking sound, and Katrina wondered if there had been more between him and Mandy than she knew.

<I'm sorry, Carl. If it's any small consolation, Anna got what she deserved.>

<I don't really want to talk about it—not now,> Carl responded after a moment. <Let's deal with this current mess first.>

<OK.> Katrina didn't know what else to say. Juasa was still staring at her with those sad, accusing eyes.

Stars...stop looking at me like that, woman!

Juasa faded away, but instead of relief, Katrina felt the hole inside of her open wider, threatening to swallow her up.

Stop it, Katrina, she admonished herself. *You made this mess—well, fucking greedy Bollers made this mess—but you need to fix it. Put Humpty Dumpty back together again...somehow.*

Katrina flipped the visual on the main display to a rear view from the *Castigation*. The ships in her flight had clustered together, in a far closer formation than would normally be safe. She could make out the docking bay doors on the *Verisimilitude* at the back of the formation—something she'd never seen unless docking at a station.

A countdown on the side of the screen noted that they were fifteen seconds from being within firing range of the BWSF cruisers.

"C'mon, Troy," Katrina whispered as the feeling of tension rose on the bridge. She was tempted to reach out to the *Voyager*, but she knew Troy had the same information they did.

Then a bright light appeared above the *'Tude*, and scan tagged it as the *Voyager*. The engine flare grew brighter then cut out, and the ship rotated, turning to face the same direction as the rest of the formation before settling down into the middle of the group.

Katrina let out a breath she hadn't realized she'd been holding. A few members of the bridge crew appeared to be doing the same thing, glancing at one another.

<*OK, we're ready,*> Sam announced to the bridge crew. <*Troy and I are controlling the shields for all the ships.*>

169

They were down to the final seconds, and the AIs didn't wait for a reply, the ships of Cavalry One extended their shields outward, layering the umbrellas over one another seconds before the enemy beams lanced out across the void.

"Shitting star balls," Jordan muttered as the shield bubble shed the enemy beams with ease. She sagged against the side of a nearby console, grinning at Katrina. "We didn't die! Stars, I've never been...I have no idea what even makes sense."

The bridge crew appeared as stunned as Jordan, and then the woman on helm let out a cry of joy that the rest of the crew took up.

Katrina found herself smiling as she looked at the shield status, seeing that they reported barely a flicker in power draw as the enemy ships continued to fire on the Midditerran formation.

"So what now?" Jordan asked as Cavalry One continued on its approach to Nesella, now only six light seconds distant.

A laugh escaped Katrina's lips. "Stars, I have no idea. I wasn't thinking past this point. We can't do much to the BWSF ships—not enough firepower—but I wonder if we can find their flagship."

<Admiral Odis is on comms,> Sam announced.

"Put him on the tank," Katrina replied, and smiled at Odis's dour face as he appeared.

"Shit, Lady Katrina, that's some maneuver you just pulled off." He sounded impressed.

Katrina laughed and nodded, the high of pure relief still flooding through her. "You have no idea, Odis. We're all pretty happy it worked."

She sent the reply and waited the ten seconds for his response.

When it came, Katrina saw him give a small smile along with a curt nod. "Well, since the alternative is that you'd be pretty much nothing, yeah, I can imagine."

Katrina shook her head, unable to help but grin back at Odis. Even though things were dire—with an extra helping of dire on the side—with Troy present, she believed they had a real chance.

"What's the situation, Odis? What's admiral Leena's ETA?"

"I've pulled in patrols, and we have a thousand ships in high orbits around Regula. We have flanking patrols ready to harry them once they engage. They're coming in fast—as are you—so we'll have a reprieve after they make their first pass. Leena has eight hundred ships incoming, but we're still outnumbered over two to one."

Katrina could see that all too well. The leading edge of the Boller fleet was moving into weapons range, and ships on both sides were trading shots at hundred thousand kilometer distances. In a few minutes, they'd be fully engaged.

"And the cantons?" Katrina asked, knowing not to hope for too much.

"There were five hundred and forty-three canton ships on Nesella that are worth the deuterium it takes to power their reactors. We have them taking up polar orbits so they have clear firing lanes that won't hit MDF ships. Kruger has also deployed his rail platforms. He had an extra twenty tucked away inside the station—the bastard."

"So he's up and about again?" Katrina asked. "I was worried about his recovery."

"Yeah, he's grumpier than before, but not that bad, I guess. I'd be pretty pissed, too, if I'd spent the last decade with an AI in my head, controlling me."

Katrina put all of the data Odis passed to her on the *Castigation*'s secondary holotank, her joy slowly fading away.

"I don't see how we can save Nesella…"

"We just saw how you saved Teegarten," Odis replied. "Given the light-lag between here and there, you must have jumped to make it this fast. Got any more tricks like that under your belt?"

Katrina wondered why Odis said 'belt', then realized it was the only actual article of clothing she was wearing other than her armor-skin.

"Funny, Odis. What about those canton ships I see coming from Persia? We don't have good scan resolution on them, but it looks like over a thousand vessels."

"Yeah, they set off before this all went down. Not sure what that's about. From a broadcast Lady Armis made, their initial goal was to 'evaluate council matters on Nesella'. They'll have fun with that, since there may not be a Nesella to evaluate when they get here."

Armis. Well, I suppose I know what's coming, if we survive this.

Katrina pushed that worry from her mind and nodded, considering the positions of the other two major

MDF fleets in the system. Both were on the far side of the star, easily five days away even if they burned through all their fuel to get to the battlespace—which would then make them useless.

"But if those canton ships could make it here before the Bollers circle around for a second pass…" Katrina mused. "Then things would be different."

"Sure, yeah," Odis snorted. "And why not summon all the other fleets in the galaxy, while we're at it."

Katrina clenched her teeth. If she didn't need Odis so much, she'd replace him in a heartbeat. Granted, his attitude was better than Myla's; at least he wouldn't do anything rash and stupid.

He probably won't do anything heroic, either.

<*What about those secret dark layer maps?*> Sam asked. <*Is there any way to get Armis's canton's ships here sooner?*>

Katrina pursed her lips. A victory where Armis was the hero would play well for the woman—and badly for Katrina.

She had half a mind to take her little group of ships and leave the system, though she'd just bring this trouble down on any system she fled to. Especially with five thousand BWSF ships on her tail.

"There's a route that would get them here…" Katrina said as she looked over the information she had lifted from Jace and Lara's minds. "Looks like…in about two hours."

"Two…" Odis stroked his chin. "That would be right as the Bollers make their second run."

Katrina didn't wait for Odis's approval. "Sam, send them the data. Tell Armis that if she gives a shit about this system, she'll take the route and save the people's asses."

"What if she thinks you're trying to do away with her?" Odis asked, clearly aware of the real purpose of Armis's fleet.

"Then we're screwed," Katrina replied. "You ready to go down fighting, Odis?"

Odis drew himself up and gave Katrina a cold look. "Do not doubt my resolve, Lady Katrina. I'm ready to give everything I have. People may call the inhabitants of Midditerra pirates, but we're not."

"Not to mention that the Bollers really aren't much better," Jordan added. "Plus, I think I resent that a bit."

Odis gave Jordan a wide grin. "Maybe we'll hash that out later."

"Maybe we will," Jordan replied.

<The message is sent,> Sam spoke up. <I sent them the whole conversation. Maybe that will convince them that we're earnest in our request.>

"Or she'll just think we faked it," Katrina said. "Either way, we have work to do. Odis, you have your end well in hand. What I want to know is whether or not you've identified their flagship. Is it one of those two-kilometer dreadnoughts?"

"Maybe," Odis said. "But all four of those are moving into the van. What I've noticed is that there's a group of cruisers hanging back. Not all the way in the rear guard, but close."

He sent the coordinates, and Katrina pulled the location up. It was a group of seven cruisers and a dozen destroyers. They were all clearly arrayed in a formation to protect one cruiser in the center.

"Whatever it is, it's important," Katrina replied.

"Agreed."

"Sam? Set a course for that ship."

<What about the formation that's attacking us right now? Our shields are holding, but every reactor in the group is running hot. Things are going to start getting really hot, really soon.>

"I'll leave you to that," Odis said. "I've got my hands full, trying to corral these canton ships and keep them out of the firing lanes for Kruger's platforms."

"Understood," Katrina replied, and Odis disappeared.

"Leading edges are now fully engaged," Jordan said as a battlespace overview filled the main tank. "Those fuckin' Bollers are trying to hit Nesella from five sides."

"Well, let's mess them up as much as we can," Katrina said. "Maximum burn."

The ships changed vector, slowing and moving toward the center-rear of the BWSF fleet. The group of cruisers that had engaged them continued to harass Cavalry One, but few other ships did, preparing as they were to engage with the bulk of the MDF fleet and the station's defenses.

<I have a question,> Troy asked.

"Fire away," Katrina replied.

<Carl tells me that the reactors on these ships store excess heat as plasma when they can't extend cooling vanes.>

"That's right," Jordan replied. "When we get the chance, we drop plasma through shield holes, but it's a big risk in battle, because the enemy can see us prepping to do that. With this many ships, they'd shoot through the opening and blow us apart."

<It's also a part of why plasma weapons are all but useless,> Sam added. <Though everyone keeps trying to invent one that works.>

<Yeah, I get that,> Troy replied. <But we're in a unique situation here. What if every ship vented plasma, and we pooled it, holding it with a-grav fields? Since we have layered shields, we could pass the plasma through them in sequence without opening ourselves up.>

"That could work," Jordan mused. "We should have Demy in on it."

<I'm already reviewing it, they ran it past me first,> Demy joined the conversation. <But I see where Troy is going with this. He's not talking venting. He's talking weaponizing.>

"I must be missing something," Katrina said, shaking her head as she turned the idea over in her mind. "We'd propel the plasma with a-grav? That would move it too slowly. How are we going to weaponize that?"

<We'll need the enemy to get very, very close,> Troy replied.

A RISK WORTH TAKING
STELLAR DATE: 02.07.8512 (Adjusted Gregorian)
LOCATION: *Castigation*
REGION: Regula, Midditerra System

Katrina's fleet formation had ceased acceleration and was drifting amongst the enemy. Each of her ships were venting plasma, which Troy was forming into a single ball on the port side of the group.

The BWSF cruisers pursuing them had closed as the Midditerrans slowed, their closest ships now within five thousand kilometers.

So far, the enemy had made no communication attempts, but Katrina knew they must be wondering if their quarry contained the prize: Katrina herself.

The enemy had ceased heavy weapons fire, but they were still tagging the shield bubble every few seconds, probing for weaknesses.

"Think they'll send assault craft?" Jordan asked.

"Stars," Katrina shook her head. "I sure hope not—for those poor bastards' sakes. We'd shoot them down in a heartbeat."

"Well, they think we're almost overheated in here—which isn't that far from the truth."

Katrina wiped her brow, momentarily forgetting that she no longer sweated—something she sorely wished was possible right now, as her body temperature continued to rise.

"Yeah, but we'd still be able to take out the first few ships."

<Boller space force isn't known for its compassion,> Sam added. <But I think they'll launch ships, and then resume heavy fire, trying to punch a hole.>

"We need to jink and hit that closest cruiser first," Katrina replied. "Do you have all the burns calculated?"

<Every ship has been checked and confirmed. We're ready to jink,> Troy replied.

Katrina glanced at Jordan, the two women sharing a worried look.

"Do it," Katrina ordered.

The ships in Cavalry One surged starboard, closing the gap with the closest BWSF cruiser to just over ten kilometers.

Before the enemy ship could react, Troy altered the shield bubble to stretch out and touch the enemy ship's shields, nullifying both fields where they made contact.

A second later, the ball of plasma that had been floating along with the ships broke into a thousand pieces, each flying across the ten-kilometer gap, striking the enemy ship. A thousand holes were burned into the BWSF cruiser's hull, venting atmosphere. Before the enemy ship could return fire, Troy pulled the shield bubble back, its protection snapping back into place.

"All ships fire!" Katrina ordered.

Every vessel in the formation fired beams at the BWSF cruiser—which had not recovered its shields—burning away hull plating and melting through dozens of decks.

A moment later, it was done. The enemy cruiser was a drifting hulk, its life support and fuel bleeding out into the void.

"Shit," Jordan whispered. "That was awesome."

It took less than ten seconds for the other BWSF cruisers to move away from the Midditerrans, none wanting the same treatment. Another glowing ball of plasma began to form within the shield bubble, waiting for another target to venture close enough.

"Resume course for that flagship," Katrina ordered. "Let's see what they do with us coming for them."

She wished she could avoid watching the main engagement around Nesella, but she knew it was her duty to at least observe. The light lag between her and the bulk of her fleet would make any directives useless by the time they arrived. She had to trust that the MDF knew what they were doing, and were prepared to put their lives on the line to protect their system.

So far, they appeared to be doing just that. Odis and the MDF had mounted a valiant defense, and the leading edge of Leena's fleet was in range, harrying the enemy as they closed with Regula.

It was a strange battle, with the fleets so spread out. Parts of the first engagement were already over, ships swept past one another, now on long braking burns as they arced around the edges of the battlespace to come back for another pass.

Dozens more ships from both sides drifted in the dark: some dead and lifeless, others burning, still more venting atmosphere, spinning on their way to oblivion.

A few ships detonated when they took too much damage, and one ship lost bottle containment, an antimatter explosion flaring out amidst the chaos.

The exploding ship was a Blackadder destroyer in close defense of Nesella. The blast hadn't damaged the station, but it had destroyed another Adder ship, along with four of the enemy.

Katrina knew that antimatter bottles were notoriously hard to breach, and suspected it was intentional. She wasn't pleased to see antimatter in use like that, but she couldn't help but approve of how the desperate defense caused the Boller ships to give Nesella a wider berth.

Even so, the station was not coming through unscathed. It was too large to shield perfectly, and BWSF beams and kinetics were breaching shields and impacting the station itself far more than Katrina had expected.

<Two minutes until we're within plasma range of the flagship,> Troy announced. <We'll also be just one minute from the MDF fleet at that point.>

Suddenly, a notion occurred to Katrina. The beginnings of an idea that could end this entire fight before it escalated further.

"Jordan! Get an assault team to meet me in the shuttle bay. We're going to pay the Bollers a visit."

"What!?" Jordan's mouth hung slack. "What are you—"

"I'm going to *end* this," Katrina replied as she rushed off the bridge.

180

THE ADMIRAL
STELLAR DATE: 02.07.8512 (Adjusted Gregorian)
LOCATION: BWSS *Nova Star*
REGION: Kora, Midditerra System

Admiral Pierson let out a low whistle as he watched the group of Midditerran ships in the interlocked shield bubble destroy a cruiser.

"That's either the smartest—or the craziest— maneuver I've ever seen," he said while shaking his head.

"Not that effective, though, sir," Major Doma replied from the other side of the holotable. "At that rate, they can destroy all of our ships in…oh, about a year."

Pierson gave a soft laugh. "I did give 'crazy' as an option. Tell FG Seventy-Two to cease pursuing that enemy formation. Let them flit about, boiling the hulls off their ships. When this is done, we'll take care of them."

Major Doma nodded and passed the order, while Pierson surveyed the rest of the battlespace. His ships were taking a pounding—the MDF and their pirate comrades were putting up a good fight. He'd feared they'd defend their system zealously, and that fear was proving true.

Many of the BWSF strategists had been convinced that the Midditerrans would flee in the face of a force the size of Pierson's, but he had disagreed.

Most systems had allies, people who would come to their aid—or at least harbor refugees. Midditerra had no such friends. If they were defeated, there was nowhere for them to flee. They'd be expelled from any nearby system they attempted to seek shelter in.

Pierson knew that the Midditerrans understood this was a battle they *had* to win.

Major Doma frowned at the battlespace, enlarging a section of the conflict. "Huh…that group in the shield bubble is coming toward us."

"Intercept?" Pierson asked.

"Close. They were already pointed in our general direction. Maybe they're just trying leave the battlespace. It's what I'd do, in their position."

Pierson cocked an eyebrow at Doma, then glanced at Colonel Reg. "Colonel. I want you to work up strike scenarios to board those ships without too much damage. There's a chance the Streamer Woman is aboard one of them."

"I'm in agreement with that assessment," Colonel Reg replied. "It's possible that ship that arrived last is her ship, too. Its hull profile has changed, but if you strip away most of the cargo pods, it is a close match."

Pierson agreed with the colonel. "Well then, all the more reason to be careful."

Pierson knew that he could very shortly be at a crossroads. His orders were to find the most expeditious means to capture the Streamer Woman—and her ship, if possible.

However, he'd already lost hundreds upon hundreds of ships. He wasn't prepared to leave his people behind once he had the woman captured. Taking this planet and station, at the very least, was a must. He also had to mount S&R operations to help Admiral Dalia retrieve her lost personnel.

No, better to have her focus on that now. There's no point in trying to take Teegarten Station anymore—though those planet pushers would be quite the prize as well.

"Doma, tell Admiral Dalia to fall back. She needs to rescue any survivors and destroy any damaged ships. No need to let these pirates salvage more military craft than they already have."

"Yes, Admiral," Doma replied.

Pierson glanced at the holo before him, considering concentrating his rear fleet elements on Nesella station rather than the MDF ships. The station housed more weapons systems than he'd expected; taking it now would remove the enemy's stronghold, and could scatter their fleets, making them easier to pick off in the second pass.

The chaos of Nesella's destruction would also benefit his endeavors. The Midditerrans could fight all they wanted, but the outcome of this battle was a foregone conclusion.

He passed the orders to the rear formations, and then looked for the small group of ships he was now all but certain held what he was seeking.

"Wait…where are they?"

"Sir?" Doma asked, looking down at the holo.

"The shield-bubbled Midditerrans. They're gone."

Doma opened her mouth to reply, when proximity alarms sounded, warning of ships within one kilometer of the *Nova Star*.

"Black night, it's them!" Doma all but shouted, as more alarms sounded, indicating that the ship had taken damage.

Pierson focused the battlespace on his flagship and saw the enemy's shield bubble pressed against the *Nova Star*. Holes from plasma strikes were venting from a hundred locations, while beams tore into his ship, disabling point defenses.

Just as suddenly as the attack had started, the enemy stopped firing.

Pierson knew what was coming next.

Sure enough, over two-dozen assault craft launched from the enemy vessels, crossing the gulf to the *Nova Star*.

"They're insane," Doma whispered.

"No. Cunning," Pierson replied, as the ship's captain called over the 1MC and shipnet, ordering all hands to prepare to repel boarders.

Pierson checked his sidearm. If the Streamer Woman had launched an attack aimed at his ship, there was only one target she would have in mind.

THE WARLORD
STELLAR DATE: 02.07.8512 (Adjusted Gregorian)
LOCATION: BWSS *Nova Star*
REGION: Kora, Midditerra System

Katrina peered around a corner and fired her rifle at the retreating enemy soldiers. One of her kinetic rounds hit a woman in the back, and she dropped to the ground.

"Advance," Katrina called back to the eight Adders with her, and they moved ahead, securing the corridor while Katrina followed behind.

<*OK, Sam we're close. Here's what I see,*> she passed the feed to the AI, who was correlating the information with what he and Demy knew of BWSF capital ship layouts.

<*Yes, you are…OK, yeah, that conduit overhead, focus on it, it should have markings…yes! Take a right at the next intersection. You should be able to see the central node from there.*>

Katrina reached the end of the corridor, where the Adders were standing over the woman Katrina had dropped.

"Shit, that sucks for her," Lloyd said, pointing at the writhing woman on the deck. "Armor fractured from the shot, and I think it broke her spine."

Katrina looked at the woman, who had stopped moving, though she was still moaning in pain.

"I'll do better next time." She flipped her rifle to pulse-mode before firing twice at the soldier's head. The point-blank pulse shot cracked her helmet, and blood began to leak out.

"Stars," one of the Adders whispered.

"No one's going to be coming for her," Katrina replied. "This was a kindness."

No one argued, and she pointed down the right-hand passage.

"That way."

The team worked their way down the passage until they reached another intersection.

<Uhh…Sam…>

<Yeah, I see what you see; doesn't look right at all.>

Katrina nodded as she peered down the passageways. *<Yeah, there's no central comm node here.>*

<Aw, crap! It's one deck up!>

"OK, folks, we've gotta head up a deck. There's a ladder shaft down that left-hand passage."

Lloyd and one of the other Adders took the lead, and Katrina followed. They were moving down the corridor at a good pace, when a shot rang out from behind them. Katrina spun to see one of the Adders in the back of the group fall.

"They're behind us!" she called out, and four of the Adders turned, firing down the passage as they picked up the pace.

Katrina zoomed her vision, spotting a half-dozen enemies at the far end of the passage. She took careful aim and squeezed off a trio of kinetic rounds. One of the enemies fell, and she took aim at another of the Bollers, firing once before the rest fell back behind cover.

"At the ladder," Lloyd called, and Katrina heard the *whump* of a conc grenade going off one deck up. She fired more rounds at the corners of the hall where the

Bollers had retreated, keeping them pinned as much as she could.

She was almost at the ladder, swapping out a magazine when one of the Bollers leant out around the corner and fired a beam down the passageway.

It brushed against her thigh, burning away most of her metal skin across a ten-centimeter patch, before hitting one of the Adders behind her.

Katrina bit back a scream and increased the frequency of her shots, waving for the other Adders to all climb the ladder first.

Seconds later, she was the last one in the passage. She lobbed a refraction grenade down the corridor before holding an arm up to her teammates.

A strong hand clamped on her wrist and pulled her up while she continued to fire rounds through the refractive haze.

"You good, Warlord?" Lloyd asked when he set her down on the deck.

Katrina looked down at her thigh, surprised to see a larger divot missing from her leg than she expected.

"Fine. Let's move," she replied with a grin.

"Are you in shock?" Lloyd asked, a look of concern visible behind his visor.

One of the Adders passed her a canister of biofoam, and she sprayed a covering over the wound. "No, it's just funny; my skin always hurts, but this might actually hurt less. Now c'mon, let's move."

If Lloyd was perturbed by the statement, it wasn't visible behind his visor as he directed two Adders to stay behind at the ladder shaft, and the rest moved twenty paces down the hall to the comm node entrance.

"This it?" Lloyd asked.

<This is,> Sam replied. <Finally.>

Katrina agreed. Getting here had been harder than she thought—and that was even with over a dozen assault teams working their way through the *Nova Star*, providing distractions and masking the true purpose of the boarding.

She placed a hand over the access panel and fed nano into the control system, bypassing the encryption systems and directly triggering the door mechanism.

"No matter how much security you put on a door, somewhere there's a physical lock and a motor that moves it," Katrina said as the door slid aside. "Just have to know where they are."

She stepped into the room that doubled as both an auxiliary comm shack, and the location of the comm NSAI. The node on the far side of the room was larger than Katrina had expected, though she surmised that it was probably because of the ship's role in the Boller Fleet.

No one was visible, though there was a half-eaten protein bar on the console, and Katrina gestured toward a corner on the far left side of the room where a cabinet lay.

Lloyd and another of the Adders strode across to the cabinet and wrenched open the doors to find a woman hiding inside. They yanked her out, and Katrina read her name tag.

"OK, Lieutenant Sarah, you're going to give me unfettered access to this system. We have some new orders to pass to your fleet."

Sarah shook her head and didn't reply, her expression scared, but defiant.

"Do you know who I am?" Katrina asked. "I'm the Streamer Woman you're all looking for. I have the technology to *make* you do what I want, and you won't like it."

As Katrina spoke, tendrils of nano formed on her metal fingertips, building up toward the woman, who began to quake with fear.

"OK, OK, what do you want?" she gasped.

"Provide your codes, and then pass the orders I give you to the rest of the fleet."

"I can't," the woman wailed. "You're going to kill them."

Katrina shook her head. "I can't really do that with orders. However, I can confuse them and force them into a retreat."

"No, no…" The woman shook her head.

"I admire your courage," Katrina said as she reached out and touched her hand to the woman's head, feeding the nano into the BWSF lieutenant's body.

Sarah screamed briefly, then her body went limp in the grip of the two Adders.

"Let her go," Katrina ordered, trying not to look at the expressions of horror on her own people's faces.

Lloyd and the other Adder released their hold, and Sarah shuffled to the console and input her access credentials. Katrina Linked with the woman's mind and provided orders that would confuse the Boller fleet, sending half their forces out of weapons range, while the others moved into vulnerable positions.

Then she passed the BWSF encryption algorithms back to Sam so he could share them with the MDF and canton ships. Now they'd have unfettered access to the BSWF comms.

"We've got company!" one of the Adders down the corridor called out.

<Damn, the BWSF has landed reinforcements from other ships. You need to get out of there,> Troy advised. <We need to break free from the Nova Star.>

"OK, team, let's get on the move," Katrina called out, signaling her Adders to knock the woman out before she relinquished control.

In the corridor, the two Adders at the ladder shaft were firing down at attackers. The deck was glowing nearby, and Katrina signaled them to fall back before the enemy melted it out from under them.

She led the Adders through the passageways, toward where their boarding ship waited.

<Are the other teams leaving?> she asked Sam.

<Yeah, they're falling back slowly, trying to buy you time. The Nova Star completely dropped shields, though. We're actually protecting the side you're on.>

Katrina checked their position in the enemy ship. "OK, team, we need to get to the end of this passageway, then down three decks and we'll almost be at our—"

<You need to double-time it!> Troy interrupted. <They just got their admiral off the ship, they're going to blow it!>

Katrina took off at run, sliding across the deck to the ladder shaft and dropping a conc down as the Adders raced after her. The grenade went off, and she swung down the shaft, dropping three decks before grabbing onto the rails and stopping herself.

She vaulted to the deck and was covering the approaches when the entire ship shuddered. She held onto the ladder as the a-grav systems went offline.

<Katrina, get—>

The ship shook again, and then white light poured through the corridor, slamming Katrina into a bulkhead. Air started racing past her. She was about to activate her magboots when another concussive wave rolled through the ship.

She lost her grip on the ladder and flew down the corridor, slamming into the bulkheads, then into a stack of conduits. Her back hit something hard enough to break ribs, and her head smashed into the deck, then everything went black.

FALLEN
STELLAR DATE: 02.07.8512 (Adjusted Gregorian)
LOCATION: *Voyager*
REGION: Regula, Midditerra System

Troy watched in horror as BWSF beams cut into the *Nova Star*, tearing the ship to shreds. He mapped their firing pattern and realized that Katrina was in the thick of it.

She wasn't going to make it off the enemy ship.

"We have to pull back," Rama said, her voice strained. "They're going to shoot right through their own ship and take us out!"

<*I can't, she's still in there,*> Troy replied, unwilling to retract the shields while Katrina was outside their protection.

"If she makes it to an assault ship, we can extend the shield around her," Carl said. "But if we all die, there's nowhere for her to go to!"

Troy spent another second considering possible options before finally agreeing with Carl's logic—logic that would likely see Katrina's end.

<*OK,*> he replied to his crew before addressing Sam and Jordan. <*I'm pulling the shield back.*>

<*I understand,*> Sam said, his voice filled with worry while Jordan cried out, "No! You can't!"

Troy was surprised by the passion in the woman's voice. She seemed to really care for Katrina.

<*We must. If we die, there will be no safe place for her.*>

Troy didn't discuss it further. Instead he drew the overlapping shield umbrellas back around Cavalry One and directed the ships to move away from the *Nova Star* as the cruisers in the BWSF formation fired on it.

As they boosted away, Troy watched a beam cut clear through the enemy's former flagship, and then another, the second one near where Katrina had been.

Come on, he thought, keeping optics and sensors trained on the breach ship she had used. Four others pulled away from the *Nova Star,* and Troy let them through the shield, barely paying attention to them once he confirmed that Katrina was not aboard.

He tried to reach her, but beamfire was striking the shield bubble now, causing too much interference for her small signal to get through.

Then the *Nova Star* exploded.

Troy had enough time to think that it must have been a self-destruct of some sort, before the shockwave hit the ships in the shield bubble and shoved them away from the Bollam's World cruisers.

Rama cried out, and Carl swore about something, but Troy wasn't paying attention. All his focus was on coordinating with Sam and keeping the shield bubble intact as the ships were thrown toward Regula's dark blue clouds.

<Manage that thrust! The formation's going to break up!> Troy ordered Sam verbally, something he rarely did when talking to other AIs.

<Trying!> Sam shot back.

Over the course of the breach, Cavalry One had moved closer and closer to the planet, holding its position relative to the enemy, as the BWSF fleet completed its initial pass, delivering strike after strike on the now-decimated Nesella station and its defensive platforms.

Troy had barely paid attention to the rest of the battlespace during the breach, but now he saw that Nesella was in ruins; millions of humans dead, as the station bled atmosphere into space.

None of that mattered now.

He refocused on his task: keeping the shields up as Sam altered vector, pushing them away from the cloud tops of Regula, even as the planet sought to pull them down into its depths.

Weathering the continual attacks and the *Nova Star*'s explosion had taxed the reactors, and two of the ships were near critical shutdown. If they fell out of position, the shield bubble would fail, and they'd either be holed by the enemy or be crushed to a pinpoint of mass.

Try as he might, there was nothing for it. They couldn't escape Regula's gravity well. As the ships slid beneath the planet's clouds, Troy shouted across the Link, willing Katrina to hear him.

<*I won't let this be our end!*>

FOUND

STELLAR DATE: 02.09.8512 (Adjusted Gregorian)
LOCATION: CDS *Talisman*
REGION: Regula, Midditerra System

Everything hurt.

A lot.

Katrina couldn't tell if she was alive or dead, just that she was in pain.

Alive then, I suppose. I don't think you can feel pain when you're dead. At least, I sure hope not.

She tried to move her body, but nothing happened. A wave of panic washed over her, but she pushed it down. Katrina tried again, and this time her hand moved.

Just exhausted…or something. Stars, my head hurts so much.

"She's coming to," a voice near her head said.

"No way. We dumped enough tranqs into her to keep a whale asleep 'til the heat death of the universe."

"The monitors don't lie."

Katrina realized she must be on a medtable. A medtable where she was being restrained.

Restrained by who?

"We need to contact Lady Armis," the first voice said. "If we try to keep her under, we might kill her."

"Armis is busy. Besides, she told us to keep her under 'til tomorrow's tribunal."

Katrina finally managed to figure out that the second voice was female, and the first was male. The male voice sounded familiar.

"Tom?" she asked weakly, still not opening her eyes.

The worry came that she was still in Revenence Castle, and that the events of the last few weeks had just been hallucinations, brought on by beatings and sunsickness.

That means Juasa is alive!

"I don't know who you're talking about, but I'm not Tom." The man's voice was wary. "Don't try anything, we have you wired up. Even think about taking over our brains, and we'll fry you like a potato."

"Seriously, Al, she's not going to—"

"Shut up, Barb. You know what she's capable of. This is the most dangerous, most brutal bitch you've ever laid eyes on. Killed her own lover just to get to Jace."

"Juasa," Katrina whispered as the pain of her love's loss crashed into her once more, making her chest feel like a giant weight was pressing down on her, squeezing the breath, the very life, from her body.

"See?" Barb said. "She's a mess. Look at that response. Can barely inhale. We've got nothing to worry about."

"We still need to call Armis," Al replied. "She'll want to know that we can't keep her sedated any longer."

"I've already called her. She's sending Korin."

Korin? Here?

Katrina wondered if it was worth opening her eyes. Korin's presence at…wherever they were…meant that she'd been betrayed.

Well, not betrayed. Katrina knew that she'd never really earned anyone's fealty.

She'd been deposed.

A laugh escaped her lips. What would Markus think of her now? A deposed dictator, probably to be taken before a tribunal and executed.

"I've become my father in every way," she whispered.

"What?" Al asked.

Katrina cracked an eyelid open to see the man standing near the wall, long pole in his hand.

"Nothing," Katrina muttered.

"Don't get any ideas," Al said. "One hit from this," he brandished the pole, "and your insides will cook."

"Fry all your nano, too," Barb said, and Katrina turned her head to see the woman standing on the other side of her, also holding a pole. At the foot of the bed were two MDF soldiers in powered armor, both holding kinetic rifles.

Katrina attempted to release a nanocloud. If she could disable the electrical prods and lock up the soldiers' armor, she'd be out in minutes.

The moment she tried, though, pain wracked her body, and she convulsed on the table.

"Sure, try to use your nano," Al grinned. "That's a new collar from Kurgise; one that you don't have the codes for. You won't be hacking your way out of this."

Katrina's head fell back.

*Apparently not. Maybe this **is** it.*

There was a sound at the foot of the bed, and Katrina lifted her head to see Korin walk in.

"I wondered if they were joking," she said quietly. "I wondered if maybe you'd show up in a situation similar to mine."

"I'm sorry, Katrina. I really am."

She could see in his eyes that Korin wasn't lying. He was genuinely sorry.

Whether or not he was sorry about what was going to happen to her, or sorry that he had to feel bad about it was less apparent.

"Lady Armis, then?" she asked.

Korin nodded. "She has a vision for a better Midditerra. One where it's not a cancerous growth, selling stolen goods and humans. You weren't going to make it better, you were just going to make it strong—and that didn't work out, either."

"Bollam's?" Katrina asked.

"They fled, what was left of them. Armis took the dark layer route and showed up just as they were falling into disarray from the comm hijack you did."

"And Nesella?" Katrina asked.

"All but destroyed. Over a hundred million dead." The accusation in Korin's voice was undisguised.

"I didn't ask for this, you know," Katrina whispered. "If Jace hadn't—"

"That doesn't matter anymore," Korin replied, his voice cold. "You've committed crimes, Katrina. Even by our laws, grievous crimes. For Armis to build a new future, you have to answer for them."

"Fine," Katrina replied. "Take me to your kangaroo court."

"It's not 'til tomorrow," Korin replied.

Katrina suddenly remembered the events of—she checked the timestamps—two days ago. "What happened to my ship, Jordan, Norm, and the rest?"

"The ships you had in that shield bubble?" Korin asked.

Katrina nodded, not liking the tone of his voice.

"When the Bollers blew the *Nova Star*, they were passing right by Regula…Jordan and the rest got pushed into the planet. They never emerged."

"Did you look for them?" Katrina asked. "You didn't, did you?

"It's still chaos out there, Katrina! There are millions of people in escape pods, half of them at risk of falling into Regula themselves! We can't go hunting for lost causes."

Katrina strained against her bonds, sneering at Korin. "You'd better hold your trials soon—either that, or just kill me now. If you leave me here for a day, I'll get free. And if I get free…."

She let the words hang, and Korin's face grew stony.

"This is the real you, isn't it?" he asked quietly. "There's no humanity inside anymore. You're just this monster."

Katrina felt the hate well up inside of her. She hated Korin, Armis, the entire Midditerra system. She even hated Juasa for dragging her heart through this mess, and Tanis for abandoning her.

Katrina hated them all.

Everyone.

"I hope you die horribly," she hissed at Korin, then screamed incoherently as Al drove his electrical prod into the wound on her leg.

"I'm really sorry it came to this," Korin said sadly. "I'd hoped when we came out here that things could end peaceably…that you'd be exiled. But—"

"Just fucking die, Korin! Die!"

Korin's face grew ashen, and he shook his head, leaving the room silently.

* * * * *

Katrina stopped paying attention to time, she didn't want to think about the minutes that were passing by, ticking closer to her death.

It was surreal to think that she'd come so close to having Troy and the *Voyager* back, only to lose them again. Of all the stupid things. She *should* have just turned on this miserable system and left when Troy and the crew arrived.

Though she tried to ignore the passage of time, Katrina did pay attention to the guards and the two medtechs—both of whom seemed more than happy to stay out of the room as much as possible.

The guards changed shifts once, and then shortly afterward, Armis arrived.

"Tomorrow already?" Katrina asked. She couldn't help but check, and saw that only five hours had passed since Korin's visit.

"No," Armis replied as she stood near the foot of the medtable, looking Katrina over. "I took your threat seriously, and we held your trial in absentia. You've been convicted of a variety of crimes. Mostly murder. Lots of murder."

Armis folded her arms as she stared down at Katrina, a deep scowl creasing her forehead. She seemed angry; whether at her own words or at Katrina's deeds, it was hard to say.

"And do I get any reprieve for all the people I saved?" Katrina asked.

"Saved? Who would that be?" Armis took a step closer, but one of the guards placed a hand on the canton leader's shoulder.

"Lady Armis, it is not wise to get close to her."

Armis shot an unreadable look at the guard, then nodded. "Right."

"Do you want a list?" Katrina asked.

"What?"

"Of the people I saved. You asked who."

"Well, I know all the people you killed."

Katrina groaned. "Midditerra is doomed with someone as stupid as you at the helm. You're complicit in the system that allowed Jace to capture me. Sloppily, I might add. So I killed him and took care of Malorie, saving the people of Revenence from slave labor in the fields. I was going to work out a plan for them to move to new crops."

"How magnanimous of you," Armis drawled. "I'll be taking over that process now."

"I hope you appreciate that it was my actions that gave you that option. I saved most of the inner system MDF fleets from Jace's clutches. Stars, I saved the whole system from that. An opportunity I was given because of

Lara's greed. Then I saved most of the people of Teegarten. Following which, I dealt the blow that broke the Bollam's World's attack."

"An attack that occurred because of your presence here," Armis shot back. "You're responsible for the deaths of over a hundred million people."

Katrina nodded solemnly. "I am. You're right. The leader is responsible. But know this, Armis. That Bollam's world fleet left for Midditerra long before they could have heard of my presence here." She let the words sink in, watching Armis's eyes grow wide before continuing.

"That means they were coming anyway. If I hadn't been free, the BWSF would have steamrolled through Midditerra and taken me by force, laying waste to everything they passed."

Armis's expression hardened once more, and she shrugged. "Maybe. Maybe not. We'll never know. All we have are the facts."

Katrina snorted. "The fact is I'm the savior of Midditerra."

"No!" Armis shot back. "You're just another cancer. *I'm* going to save this system. You're going to be pushed out an airlock, then burned to ash by my ship's beams."

"Fine," Katrina growled. "Let's just get it over with."

EXPUNGED
STELLAR DATE: 02.09.8512 (Adjusted Gregorian)
LOCATION: CDS *Talisman*
REGION: Regula, Midditerra System

Katrina stood in the airlock, waiting for the outer door to open, for the nightmare to finally end.

She was ready. Juasa was dead, and all her allies had abandoned her.

It's over.

Armis would be the new ruler of the Midditerra System. Given Katrina's performance, that would likely be for the best.

A minute passed, and the outer door stayed closed.

Katrina wondered what was taking them so long. Maybe someone just wanted to make her sweat before they finished her off.

I'm sorry, Juasa. I'm sorry I didn't listen to you. Sorry I betrayed what we had. We should have left on the Castigation *like you said. I'd —*

Katrina's thoughts were interrupted by a flash of light in the airlock. For a moment, she wondered if it was something the depressurization had done to her eyes. She'd never heard of that effect, but...

Her vision began to adjust, and she realized it wasn't a flash of light, it *was* light. There was a bright light in front of her, drifting in the space between her and the outer airlock door.

"What...?" she said softly, reaching a hand out toward it.

"You've made a lot of mistakes," the light said.

Katrina heard the words, but she wasn't certain if her ears had been involved. The sound was like a wind blowing over a plain, grass whipping to and fro, a high-pitched hiss over a low rustling.

It made her feel cold and alone, like she was surrounded by nothing but this singular force. A force against which all of her efforts were futile.

"Who are you?" Katrina asked, barely able to comprehend that the thing before her had been the speaker.

Another hallucination. I'm going insane. My mind is ruined by grief...or something...

"You're not going insane," the windy voice said, the words whispering their way into her mind. "Touch me."

Katrina realized that though she had begun to reach out to the light, her hand had stopped, trembling in place.

"What are you?" Katrina asked again.

"Touch me," the voice whispered again, the wind punctuated by a peal of thunder in the distance.

Katrina reached out and touched the thing before her. At first it felt solid, like hard light riding the surface of an electrostatic field, but then her hand slipped through and it felt warm, comforting.

"What—?"

"I am Xavia," the being said. "I have come to you, because your work is not yet done."

Katrina couldn't help but laugh. "Oh it's done alright. I don't know if you noticed, but my people are about to space me. That's about as 'done' as you can get."

A part of Xavia moved, and Katrina wondered if the being was shaking her head. "They are not your people. Your people are coming for you. They're nearly here, but you need to remain strong."

"Why?" Katrina asked. "Why should I stay strong?"

"Because," the being of light replied. "If you persevere, you'll meet Tanis again. I promise this."

Katrina's eyes widened. "No...how do you—? I *am* hallucinating.... The airlock has opened, and this is my brain dying, freezing in hard vacuum, trying to make sense of it all."

"Look beyond me," Xavia said, and Katrina leant to the side and looked beyond the being.

She gasped, realizing that the airlock door *was* open, she should be exposed to cold, hard vacuum.

Katrina sucked in a deep breath in surprise, then blew it out, knowing that when the vacuum hit, holding in air would blow her lungs apart.

Not that it mattered; she wasn't going to survive anyway. Maybe a quick death would be better.

"Relax," Xavia said. "I'm holding the air in. You're not going to die. Remember, I need you to meet with Tanis, and she's not going to arrive for some time."

"I don't understand," Katrina said, a frown creasing her features.

"You will," Xavia replied. "First, I need to fix you. You're broken. Inside and out."

Katrina nodded slowly. That was more than true. She was standing more out of force of will than anything else.

"Be strong," Xavia whispered.

A moment later, Katrina felt as though the hand touching the light-being was on fire, her every nerve ending screaming in agony.

"This is your penance," Xavia said, as Katrina pulled her hand free and watched the steel armor that was her skin begin to melt off and pool on the deck.

She thought her entire hand would disintegrate as well, but the change stopped at her exposed muscles. She couldn't help but flex her fingers, staring in terrified wonder at the macabre sight before her. Sinews and muscles stretching over bone, blood throbbing through veins in a slow rhythm.

"You did this once before," Xavia said. "You turned yourself into a monster to combat monsters. Now I'm turning you back into a woman so you can live amongst humans again."

More of the armor began to melt off Katrina's body, and she screamed in agony as her nerves were shredded, muscles and bones exposed.

"You think you deserve this," Xavia's voice was like bolts of lightning in Katrina's mind, a sharp crack followed by a thundering boom, the very sound of it shaking her body. "You're not wrong. You *have* earned this, but know that this penance is not all you need. The dead cannot absolve you. I cannot absolve you. The living, the people you thought were your allies, they have exacted their punishment by sentencing you to death.

"Now you must forgive yourself."

"I can't!" Katrina wailed as she watched the armor-skin slough off her chest, exposing her sternum. Through thin muscle stretched across her ribs, the form of her heart was visible beneath, pushing against bone and sinew. Katrina screamed in agony, unable to close her eyes, unable to cry.

"You must!" Xavia insisted. "I chose you for this, Katrina. I chose you because I *know* what strength you have within you. The road ahead is going to be long and hard. More than you know—but you'll have passed through this, the crucible."

Katrina was lost in the agony that wracked her body. She was unable to speak, unable to form thoughts. All that remained was the pain, and Xavia's voice, whispering into her mind, explaining what had come before, what would come to pass, and what Katrina must do.

All that Katrina could see was Xavia's light. She had no more eyelids, nothing protected her mind and body from the being before her. The being that was ruining her to offer salvation.

Then a strange feeling came to her right hand, the hand that had touched the light. Katrina didn't understand it at first, but then she realized what it was.

There's no pain.

She looked down and saw skin on her hand. Perfect, unblemished skin.

It began to appear on her arm, on her chest, across her entire body. Her breasts grew back, her navel formed, soft hair on her stomach standing up in the cold air.

She held up her hand to see fingernails regrow, and then felt a tickling on her scalp and knew hair was growing out from her head.

She blinked, skin sliding over her eyes. An amazing delight—she had almost forgotten what it felt like.

"I'm me again," Katrina whispered, running her hands across her body, tears welling in her eyes.

"You were always you," Xavia replied. "You just forgot who that was. You touch all these things, you live in their worlds. But you are not them, and they are not you. You are Katrina."

Katrina's chest constricted, and she gulped a deep breath, tears streaming from her eyes.

"I am Katrina," she whispered.

"Louder," Xavia replied.

"I am *Katrina*."

"Believe it."

"I. Am. Katrina!"

"Good. Now go. I have work for you."

Suddenly the light was gone, and all that lay before Katrina was the starlit expanse of space, waiting for her beyond the yawning portal of the airlock.

For a moment, Katrina wondered what would happen. Would the inner door open once more? Would she go back onto Armis's ship?

Then something snapped, and the air exploded out into space, taking Katrina with it.

ESCAPE
STELLAR DATE: 02.09.8512 (Adjusted Gregorian)
LOCATION: *Voyager*
REGION: Regula, Midditerra System

It had taken excruciatingly precise burns to slow the ships, and then begin to crawl out of Regula's depths. Only Troy's extensive experience with managing long burns in adverse conditions had managed to keep the formation in shape.

Troy completed a final burn, and the ships reached the planet's upper atmosphere, only a few-dozen kilometers below the cloud tops.

<What do you think has happened out there?> Sam asked, using words for the benefit of the humans in the conversation.

Troy was optimistic—at least about the battle's outcome. <I believe the Midditerrans won the day. Losing the BWSF flagship and having their fleet spread about in disarray should have been enough to make the enemy abandon this venture—so long as Armis brought that other fleet into play.>

"Well, we're seconds away from an altitude where we can pick up comm traffic, so we'll know soon enough," Captain Jordan spoke over the open channel.

Troy was ready to pore through every signal out there, searching for whatever he could find about Katrina. When he tapped into the traffic a minute later, it turned out to be easier than he thought.

<They found her!> he announced, unrestrained glee in his voice fading as he realized what Katrina's rescuers

had done. <*And they convicted her and sentenced her to death.*>

"What the hell?" Norm asked. "She's the one who saved the day! I assume she saved the day, right? It's not the Bollers we're talking about, right?"

<*No,*> Sam replied. <*Her tactic worked. The Bollers retreated. They've left the system.*>

"What in the stars are they trying her for?" Jordan asked.

<*Everything,*> Troy replied. <*On the orders of President Armis.*>

" 'President'?"

It sounded to Troy like Jordan was going to choke.

<*Yes, that is the rank her official communication—oh no…*> Troy paused, <*No, they're going to carry out her execution in minutes—just tossing her out an airlock!*>

"How far are they?" Jordan asked. "Max burn, give me max burn!"

<*There,*> Sam said, placing Armis's ship on the *Castigation*'s holo relative to the Cavalry One's position inside Regula's clouds.

Suddenly a voice came into Troy's mind, one he didn't recognize. <*I'll blind their sensors.*>

<*And you are?*> Troy asked, momentarily worried that Katrina's would-be murderers had found them.

<*A friend. They won't see you coming, but you must hurry. Be ready to take her in.*>

Troy couldn't identify the origin of the signal; it seemed to be coming from a half-dozen locations at once. After the words, coordinates came—a location on the starboard side of a ship listed as the *Talisman*.

<I have a location on Katrina,> Troy said to the commanders, not caring who was helping, so much as that they were. *<Katrina will be there.>*

"How do you know?" Jordan asked, and Troy could see doubt on her face through the *Castigation*'s bridge optics.

<Someone told me. I don't know for sure to trust them…but we're boosting out of the clouds anyway.>

Jordan gave a cold laugh. "True, good to have a goal for our suicide run."

Katrina's fleet—as Troy now thought of it—burst from Regula's cloud tops, thrusting at over ten *g*s toward Armis's vessel.

It was a sizable cruiser, nearly as big as the *Castigation*, but it was dwarfed by the closely grouped ships on approach. Troy expected to see the *Talisman*'s weapons come online and begin to target Cavalry One, but the enemy ship wasn't responding to their approach at all.

"What the…?" Carl muttered from his seat in the *Voyager*'s cockpit. "It's like they don't see us."

<This friend said they'd be blind to us,> Troy shared. *<I guess it was no lie.>*

"The other ships, too," Norm joined the conversation. "No one has activated weapons, that I can see, no course alterations to intercept us. This is weird."

<I see an open airlock,> Sam announced. *<Right where your coordinates said, Troy.>*

<Whoever that is, she's pulling off a miracle.>

"She?" Jordan asked.

<Felt female,> Troy replied. *<Hard to say, though…>*

Jordan frowned and glanced up at the optical pickups on her bridge. "So it was a human?"

<*I—I don't really know. I'm not questioning it right now. We were rushing headlong into danger regardless.*>

"Good point."

The ships crossed the half a light second of space between Regula and the *Talisman*, and Troy readied an opening in the shield bubble, preparing to use an a-grav beam to pull Katrina in.

"If the airlock is open, where is she?" Carl asked.

"I bet they're tormenting her with a shield over the door." Rama sounded angry, more than Troy would have expected. He wondered if someone had once done something like that to her in the past.

<*No matter, when we get in range, I can hit the airlock with a grav beam and nullify their shield.*>

"Suck her right out of their ship." Carl nodded in approval. "I like it."

No one spoke for the next minute as they continued to boost toward the *Talisman*. Then, ten seconds before Troy was ready to reach out and grab Katrina, he saw a puff of atmosphere explode from the airlock, followed by a body.

<*Shit!*> he exclaimed, and stretched out the grav beam, pulling her toward them. <*Camille, Kirb, I'm bringing her into our ship. Get her to med as soon as she's in!*>

<*Bay door's open,*> Camille replied from below.

Troy fed the grav beam through the shield bubble, carefully grabbing Katrina's body and pulling it toward the ship. The relative velocity of the *Voyager* and the other ships in the formation was such that he had to take great care not to crush her body.

Somehow, through a skill Troy did not know he possessed, he succeeded.

<*I've got her!*> he called out across the small fleet, pulling Katrina across kilometers of vacuum as quickly as he dared. Her body was motionless, and he feared she might be dead, but IR showed heat, and that gave him hope.

Then she was through the shield and inside the *Voyager's* bay.

<*Is she alive?*> Troy asked. <*Tell me! Is she?*>

<*Hold,*> Camille shot back. <*Yes, yes, she's alive. And she has skin! What the—nevermind! Getting her to medical!*>

Troy wished he had lungs—it felt like he'd just held his breath for the entire maneuver, and he wanted to gasp with relief.

<*You're welcome,*> the unidentified voice said.

<*Who are you? Why did you do this?*> Troy was almost desperate to learn who had done so much to save Katrina.

<*Take good care of her, Troy. She's important.*>

Then the connection was gone, and Troy was left only with supposition.

"We're getting out of this system," Jordan announced. "All ships, coordinate burns with Sam. Midditerra is in our past."

Troy wondered if the MDF and canton captains would argue with Jordan, but none did. Over the last three days, the humans had formed a camaraderie built around Katrina. One that he didn't understand, but was glad worked in his favor.

<All ships ready to burn on outsystem vector,> Sam announced. <Where to, Captain Jordan?>

Jordan laughed and shook her head. "First star on the left and straight on 'til morning."

<Uh...Jordan?> Sam asked. <Seriously?>

"New Eden, Sam. Take us to New Eden."

KATRINA
STELLAR DATE: 02.09.8512 (Adjusted Gregorian)
LOCATION: *Voyager*
REGION: Edge of the Midditerra System

Katrina woke with a start, sitting bolt upright in her bed.

"What the...?" she asked, looking around at her surroundings, taking a moment to identify it as her cabin aboard the *Voyager*.

<*You're safe, Katrina,*> Troy's voice entered her mind over a local Link.

She drew a deep, pain-free breath and held up her hand, marveling at seeing soft, pink skin, and flexing her fingers without any discomfort.

The joy at seeing her own body pure and unmarred brought tears to her eyes, and Katrina couldn't stop a sob from breaking free from her throat.

She swallowed, struggling to keep her emotions under control. "Stars...what...was that all a dream?"

<*Which part? The part where you took control of a whole star system and then led a suicide mission against a Bollam's World cruiser, or the part where you got shot out of an airlock, miraculously healed?*>

A laugh escaped Katrina's throat, but she couldn't bring herself to speak the question in her mind.

Or the part where I fell in love with an amazing woman and then lost her through my own actions...?

After a moment, she replied aloud. "I guess…based on your question, that it was all real. Even the part with *her*."

< *'Her'? The one who helped us?>* Troy asked. *<Who was she?>*

"How do you know about her?" Katrina asked.

<Well, 'about' is a strong word. Someone contacted me, told me where to find you. We pulled you in right after you were shot out of the airlock.>

"Stars…she was something. Something else. A being of light."

<Is she the one who gave you your skin back? I can't see Armis doing that.>

Katrina laughed at the thought, reveling in the ability to laugh without pain.

No physical pain, at least.

She swung her legs over the edge of her bed and rose carefully, reveling in the feeling of her bare feet pressing into the deck, feeling the small ridges of the surface.

Katrina scrunched her toes, almost crying out for joy at how good it felt to just *move*.

She turned toward the door to her cabin, not sure where she was going, but wanting to be with people—to feel human around them once more.

<Uh…Katrina?> Troy asked.

"Yeah?"

<You're naked.>

Katrina looked down at herself and laughed. "Whoops! You know, other than a coat, I haven't worn clothes in months."

<Well, now's probably a good time to pick up the habit again. You're practically glowing, and if Kirb gives you a second look, Camille is going to hit him.>

Katrina laughed again, still loving the feel of it. Loving the sound of it. Bit by bit, the pain of what she'd been through was lessening. Not going away, but lessening.

"I could laugh all day," she said quietly to herself as she turned to her closet and selected a simple shipsuit with the *Intrepid*'s logo emblazoned over her heart.

<Much better. Ready to face the world?>

"Just a minute," Katrina replied as she stood in the middle of her cabin and stretched her arms above her head.

After holding the stretch for a few seconds, she began her mantra.

"I am Katrina," she whispered. "Daughter of the despot Yusuf, friend of the Noctus, liberator of the *Hyperion*, wife of Markus, president of Victoria, searcher in the dark. I am the lover of Juasa, the survivor of the fields, despot of Midditerra…. And once again, searcher in the dark."

She breathed out, closed her eyes, and breathed in once more. "I am all of those things, together they are me. They form my foundation, they give me purpose, my memories are my strength, the proof of my convictions."

She bowed her head, touching her chin to her sternum and continued her recitation.

"I am the soft reed that grows along the shore. One foot in the river, one on land. I bend in the wind, I weather the flood, I persist, I survive. I touch all these things, I live in their worlds, but they are not me, and I am not them. My beliefs and persistence are my absolution. I am *still* Katrina."

As she spoke, Katrina placed her legs together and stretched her arms overhead, imagining herself as the flexible, unbroken reed. She bent over backward, arching her back more and more until her hands reached her ankles, then the floor.

"And even though my world may so often seem upside down," she kicked her right leg out and up, followed by her left, now standing on her hands, "it does not change who I am. I will continue to be Katrina. I am always myself; nothing less, nothing more."

She held the pose for a minute, concentrating on her breathing, before flexing her arms and pushing off, flipping through the air and landing on her feet.

She walked to the door and palmed it open.

"Now I'm ready."

THE END

* * * * *

Katrina's journey continues for many years, she continues to search in the darkness, and eventually finds that which she has sought for so long.

Katrina makes a brief appearance in Orion Rising, and eventually comes home in Attack on Thebes.

If you've not read The Orion War series, you can start with Destiny Lost, and see how Tanis and Katrina's paths—though separate for many years—weave back together.

THANK YOU

If you've enjoyed reading The Woman Who Lost Everything, a review on Amazon.com and/or goodreads.com would be greatly appreciated.

To get the latest news and access to free novellas and short stories, sign up on the Aeon 14 mailing list: www.aeon14.com/signup.

M. D. Cooper

THE BOOKS OF AEON 14

Keep up to date with what is releasing in Aeon 14 with the free Aeon 14 Reading Guide.

The Intrepid Saga (The Age of Terra)
- Book 1: Outsystem
- Book 2: A Path in the Darkness
- Book 3: Building Victoria

- The Intrepid Saga Omnibus – *Also contains Destiny Lost, book 1 of the Orion War series*

- Destiny Rising – *Special Author's Extended Edition comprised of both Outsystem and A Path in the Darkness with over 100 pages of new content.*

The Orion War
- Book 1: Destiny Lost
- Book 2: New Canaan
- Book 3: Orion Rising
- Book 4: The Scipio Alliance
- Book 5: Attack on Thebes
- Book 6: War on a Thousand Fronts (May 2018)
- Book 7: Fallen Empire (2018)
- Book 8: Airtha Ascendancy (2018)
- Book 9: The Orion Front (2018)
- Book 10: Starfire (2019)
- Book 11: Race Across Time (2019)
- Book 12: Return to Sol (2019)

Tales of the Orion War
- Book 1: Set the Galaxy on Fire
- Book 2: Ignite the Stars

- Book 3: Burn the Galaxy to Ash (2018)

Perilous Alliance (Age of the Orion War - with Chris J. Pike)
- Book 1: Close Proximity
- Book 2: Strike Vector
- Book 3: Collision Course
- Book 4: Impact Imminent (April 2018)

Rika's Marauders (Age of the Orion War)
- Prequel: Rika Mechanized
- Book 1: Rika Outcast
- Book 2: Rika Redeemed
- Book 3: Rika Triumphant
- Book 4: Rika Commander (April 2018)
- Book 5: Rika Unleashed (2018)
- Book 6: Rika Infiltrator (2018)
- Book 7: Rika Conqueror (2019)

Perseus Gate (Age of the Orion War)
Season 1: Orion Space
- Episode 1: The Gate at the Grey Wolf Star
- Episode 2: The World at the Edge of Space
- Episode 3: The Dance on the Moons of Serenity
- Episode 4: The Last Bastion of Star City
- Episode 5: The Toll Road Between the Stars
- Episode 6: The Final Stroll on Perseus's Arm
- Eps 1-3 Omnibus: The Trail Through the Stars
- Eps 4-6 Omnibus: The Path Amongst the Clouds

Season 2: Inner Stars
- Episode 1: A Meeting of Bodies and Minds
- Episode 3: A Deception and a Promise Kept (2018)
- Episode 3: A Surreptitious Rescue of Friends and Foes (2018)
- Episode 4: A Trial and the Tribulations (2018)

- Episode 5: A Deal and a True Story Told (2018)
- Episode 6: A New Empire and An Old Ally (2018)

Season 3: AI Empire
- Episode 1: Restitution and Recompense (2019)
- Five more episodes following...

The Warlord (Before the Age of the Orion War)
- Book 1: The Woman Without a World
- Book 2: The Woman Who Seized an Empire
- Book 3: The Woman Who Lost Everything

The Sentience Wars: Origins (Age of the Sentience Wars - with James S. Aaron)
- Book 1: Lyssa's Dream
- Book 2: Lyssa's Run
- Book 3: Lyssa's Flight
- Book 4: Lyssa's Call (2018)
- Book 5: Lyssa's Flame (2018)

Enfield Genesis (Age of the Sentience Wars - with Lisa Richman)
- Book 1: Alpha Centauri (2018)

Machete System Bounty Hunter (Age of the Orion War - with Zen DiPietro)
- Book 1: Hired Gun
- Book 2: Gunning for Trouble (May 2018)
- Book 3: With Guns Blazing (2018)

Vexa Legacy (Age of the FTL Wars - with Andrew Gates)
- Book 1: Seas of the Red Star

Fennington Station Murder Mysteries (Age of the Orion War)

- Book 1: Whole Latte Death (w/Chris J. Pike)
- Book 2: Cocoa Crush (w/Chris J. Pike)

The Empire (Age of the Orion War)
- The Empress and the Ambassador (2018)
- Consort of the Scorpion Empress (2018)
- By the Empress's Command (2018)

Tanis Richards: Origins (The Age of Terra)
- Prequel: Storming the Norse Wind (At the Helm Volume 3)
- Book 1: Shore Leave (June 2018)
- Book 2: The Command (June 2018)
- Book 3: Infiltrator (July 2018)

The Sol Dissolution (The Age of Terra)
- Book 1: Venusian Uprising (2018)
- Book 2: Scattered Disk (2018)
- Book 3: Jovian Offensive (2019)
- Book 4: Fall of Terra (2019)

The Delta Team Chronicles (Expanded Orion War)
- A "Simple" Kidnapping (Pew! Pew! Volume 1)
- The Disknee World (Pew! Pew! Volume 2)
- It's Hard Being a Girl (Pew! Pew! Volume 4)
- A Fool's Gotta Feed (Pew! Pew! Volume 4)
- Rogue Planets and a Bored Kitty (Pew! Pew! Volume 5)

ABOUT THE AUTHOR

Michael Cooper likes to think of himself as a jack-of-all-trades (and hopes to become master of a few). When not writing, he can be found writing software, working in his shop at his latest carpentry project, or likely reading a book.

He shares his home with a precocious young girl, his wonderful wife (who also writes), two cats, a never-ending list of things he would like to build, and ideas...

Find out what's coming next at www.aeon14.com

Made in the USA
San Bernardino, CA
03 November 2018